# WHEN DEAD IN GREECE

## JACK NOBLE BOOK FIVE

## L.T. RYAN

LIQUID MIND MEDIA

# THE JACK NOBLE SERIES

*The Recruit (free)*
*The First Deception (Prequel 1)*
*Noble Beginnings*
*A Deadly Distance*
*Ripple Effect (Bear Logan)*
*Thin Line*
*Noble Intentions*
*When Dead in Greece*
*Noble Retribution*
*Noble Betrayal*
*Never Go Home*
*Beyond Betrayal (Clarissa Abbot)*
*Noble Judgment*
*Never Cry Mercy*
*Deadline*
*End Game*

Receive a free copy of The Recruit by visiting http://ltryan.com/newsletter.

# 1

PALAIOCHORA, GREECE.

OLD MEN CROWDED the white-tiled terrace. They gathered at the cafe once a week for their backgammon tournament. They made bets. Talked trash. Winked at the waitress. Conned free coffee out of the establishment's owner. A few minutes after their arrival the aroma of dark roast overtook the adjoining Libyan Sea.

This was the first time I'd managed to stand long enough to watch the initial round of matches. I'd spent my first two weeks in Palaiochora on my back, recovering from my injuries. A collapsed lung. Bruised spleen. Hairline fractures to my jaw, right ulna, both tibias. Several broken ribs to go along with broken bones in my left hand.

The majority of the injuries had been sustained during a nasty fight with my seven-foot-tall Russian cellmate in the hell-hole named Black Dolphin. The guards of that fine place were kind enough to do the rest of the damage.

Then there was the manner of how I escaped. Wasn't my own doing. But, damn, did the effects linger on.

Over the past month the physical pain had subsided. I still wasn't myself though. Fatigue set in fast. My strength was sapped. Mental acuity was nowhere near what I was used to. I presumed these were the side effects of whatever the Russian, Alik, had slipped me to send me into that deep slumber. It was hard to be angry with the guy. He'd only done what Frank Skinner had instructed him to do. And he'd managed to get me out of that shithole prison.

Life, and death, sentence served.

Half the old guys cheered as the final match of the first round wrapped up. They stood feet wide, hands up, palms slapped, as the losers pulled bills from their wallets and handed them over to the victors. The next stop for the old men was inside to replenish their food stores and refill with caffeine before the next round began.

So I stepped into the cafe first to beat them to the counter.

Isadora Georgiou stood behind the glass display case that housed a selection of breakfast pastries this time of day. Her fingers danced playfully along the stainless top. She tucked a strand of dark curly hair behind her ear. Her full lips spread into a smile when she saw me approaching. A spotless apron covered her jeans and faded red t-shirt, cinched tight at the waist and loose around her breasts and hanging off her hips. She was the kind of woman who was beautiful without a trace of makeup. There wasn't so much as the thread of a wrinkle on her face.

"Looking good today, Jack." If velvet had a tone, it was her voice.

The old men settled in line behind me. Their chatter quieted to a hum.

"Not as handsome as these gentlemen, though," I said to her.

She exaggerated a shrug with upturned hands and pouty lips. "True. You are not to blame, though. Not your fault you weren't born Greek."

A couple of the old guys got a chuckle out of her comments. One said something I couldn't understand. Presumably, the comment had been inappropriate, because Isadora chided him and sent him away with a discarding wave of her hand.

"Aye, these men." She tossed her hands into the air in mock exasperation. Smiling, she turned to me. "I know what you want, Jack. I'll bring it to you after I take care of them."

I retreated to a table and watched as Isadora and her uncle, Esau Rokos, handled the rush. Esau owned the place. For a while in the 80s, he split time between the States and Greece, running a chain of Greek diners in Virginia, near D.C. This cafe, as he explained it, was his retirement. Together, Esau and Isadora slung coffee, pastries, a few orders of eggs and lamb. One at a time, the old men hustled back to the terrace to eat and resume their game.

Ten minutes later, Isadora carried a steaming plate and a fresh mug of java to me. It smelled so good I could taste it before she set it down. She asked me if I needed anything else, then took a hiatus in the back office. I watched as she crossed the room, walking away from me, her hips swaying slightly. As her ass entranced me, I realized how thankful I was that the events at Black Dolphin hadn't robbed me of my appreciation of the female form.

The door shut behind her, and I turned my attention to the food on the table. The smell of eggs fried in butter and sautéed lamb enveloped me. I dug in.

The little town had grown on me. Relaxed me. A bit quiet for my tastes. But the folks were friendly. Everyone seemed to know each other. The smells and sounds of the sea were ever-present. Reminded me a bit of where I grew up.

Alik and I weren't sure how long we would have to stay in Greece. Only thing Frank had said was to stay put. He would send for me when he needed me. There would be no advanced notice. Until then, Alik watched over me, and I watched Isadora and the old men and the others who frequented the cafe.

*Take your time, Frank,* I thought. *No rush.*

"You really do look better." Isadora walked past me and stopped on the other side of the table. I hadn't noticed her approaching. Was I losing my edge, or was the food that good? Her perfume trailed after her. Smelled like lavender. My mother grew the herb by the dozens, and in several varieties. Couldn't walk in the house without smelling it. Isadora folded her arms over the back of the chair and leaned toward me. The legs of the chair scraped against the tile. "Almost look like you could throw a ball around. That's what you Americans like to do, yeah? Football and baseball and stuff."

"Something like that." I drained the remaining coffee from my mug and started to stand. "Anyway, coming back to life is harder than they make it look in the movies."

She gave me an odd look, then reached out and wrapped her slender hand around my arm. Her touch felt cool.

"I can take that for you," she said

"I need the exercise," I said.

"Stubborn man," she said.

"As opposed to what?" I said.

She winked and smiled and turned toward the counter. I waited a couple beats, then followed in her scented wash. She must've reapplied the perfume while in the office because I hadn't noticed earlier. Or perhaps I'd been too hungry so only the smell of food filtered in. Either way, I couldn't blame the lady for wanting to smell as nice as she looked.

Watching her round the counter, I paid little attention to the jingling as the front door opened, and hard soles slapping the tile behind me. But the person stopped too close. I glanced over and saw a guy about my age, a wide nose in the middle of a face covered with stubble. He was dressed in black trousers, a white button up, and wore dark sunglasses.

His shoulder hit the center of my back. His elbow and forearm found the tender spot on my ribs. I don't know if he got his leg in front of mine, or if I stumbled over myself. But I went down.

Hard.

First into the display case, then the floor.

The mug crashed on the tile and splintered into a hundred pieces. Ceramic shards flew in all directions. Several hit me in the face. One felt like it did a little damage.

"Get out of my damn way," the guy said, his accent deep and thick.

Isadora spun, her arms wide. She leaned over the counter and looked down at me. "Are you OK?"

I nodded as I planted my hands on the floor and pushed my torso up. The guy had continued walking past me. He entered the office. A minute later he returned, walked past me again on his way to the front door.

Isadora vaulted over the counter and headed toward the front door, firing off a torrent of words I didn't understand.

The man kicked the door open. The bells jingled all at once. He kept the door propped open with his right arm, glanced over his left shoulder.

He said, "*Psolapothiki.*"

I wasn't sure of the literal translation, but knew he called her the equivalent of a *whore*. The insult stopped her. She looked back at me. Her face darkened and she turned to the front of the cafe again. She aimed an outstretched finger at the guy, then stormed toward him.

"Isa!" Esau's voice filled the cafe. His thinning white hair was disheveled. One cheek was redder than the other. Blood spotted the corner of his mouth. "Stop."

The guy at the door chuckled, said something I didn't catch, then left.

## 2

RANDOM PEOPLE ATTEMPTING TO GET THE BEST OF ME WAS nothing new. Seemed to happen wherever I went. Maybe it was the way I looked. The confidence I exuded. Someone always wants to take down the alpha dog. But most of the time I went somewhere for a reason. A mission. A job. Whatever.

That wasn't the case in Greece. Aside from Frank and Alik, no one knew I was here. Hell, no one else knew I was alive. Frank had even withheld the information from his superiors in Washington, D.C.

So why had this guy targeted me? Judging by the look of Esau, who now slumped over the counter, I figured I'd been in the way. He was the target. Not me.

I winced at the pain as I rose to my feet. Felt as though the guy had nailed me with a sap instead of his elbow. Might have. Damn ribs had almost healed, too.

Isadora stared at the front door like she expected it to burst open any second now. Her anger hadn't faded. She looked more pissed now than she had before her uncle yelled out to her. After a few seconds she turned and walked toward me. The anger on her face dissipated. Her eyes and lips softened. She reached and placed her hand on my elbow. Her touch wasn't as cool as it had been earlier.

"You OK?" I asked her.

"Me?" She stopped and looked me up and down. Reached out and touched my cheek. Her finger came away crimson. "You're the one that took a beating."

I shrugged, jutted my chin toward her uncle. "Don't think I got the worst of it."

"Uncle," she said, brushing against me chest-to-chest as she sidestepped past. Strands of her hair caught and lingered for a second before being tugged away. "What's going on? What did he do to you?"

Esau fought off her attempts at assisting.

"Quit being so stubborn, you old fool." She threaded her arm around his back and eased him into a chair.

Esau grimaced as he leaned back into his seat. A tiny stream of blood trickled from his lip and down his chin. He dabbed it with a napkin, then looked at the red patch as though it were an old friend he'd nearly forgotten existed.

Isadora had retreated behind the counter. She filled a bag with ice and wrapped a towel around it. I took it over to Esau. He held it to his cheek and closed his eyes and leaned his head back.

"What happened?" I asked.

He lifted his right eyelid and watched me for a moment. "Don't know what you mean."

"You gonna tell me that you walked into a door next?"

Esau closed his eye and said nothing. A ragged exhale slipped from his mouth. Stagnant hot breath reached me.

"Who was that guy?" I said. "Don't recall seeing him in here before. Thought I'd seen most of the town at one point or another."

"He was nobody," Esau said.

"You're a horrible liar, old man."

He muttered something in Greek, leaned forward, placed the blood-soiled napkin on the table. "I let you and your Russian friend stay here. I don't ask no questions, even though it's obvious something happened to you. Why can't you give me that same respect?"

I raised my hands in surrender. "Just seeing if I can be of help, Esau. That's all."

"Well I don't need your help." He stood and stumbled toward the office.

I glanced toward Isadora. She watched her uncle retreat. I waited a moment for the office door to shut, then approached her.

"What's going on here?" I said.

She sighed. "My uncle, he's…I'm not sure how to put it."

"In trouble?"

She studied me for a moment, perhaps deciding how far to let me in. She inhaled sharply. "I think you should honor his request and stop asking questions."

"Look, I'm just saying if you need help…"

She turned away from me and feigned busy work.

I took the hint and stepped out onto the terrace where the old men still gathered. If not for a couple curious glances, I would've thought they'd played through the entire incident. Were they concerned for Esau? Shamed at seeing me knocked over? Embar-rassed because they didn't do anything to help? I nodded at those who glanced in my direction, then walked past and leaned against the railing. The waves were about waist-high and hammered the shoreline. Salt spray coated the wall below me in a fine mist. The steady breeze dried the sweat that coated my face and arms.

After a few minutes of staring out over the sea, I reentered the cafe and took a seat against the far wall. Isadora ignored me. Just as well. My heart rate had barely come down since being knocked to the floor. A sure sign I'd had enough coffee.

Most of the old guys came in, too. They'd made it through another round of matches. While some were winners, others were out of their weekly gambling stipend. They grabbed a snack or a drink or a mug and seated themselves at various tables. Chatter rose and filled the cafe. Took the chill out of the place. Felt like normal again. Sort of.

The front door opened, creating a wind tunnel for the salty breeze. Napkins lifted off tables and spiraled toward the door.

Alik stepped in. He nodded at Isadora, then walked up to me. If Esau was a bad liar, then I was even worse at hiding the fact something had happened.

"What's going on?" Alik said.

"Nothing much," I said.

"You've got a cut on your face."

I'd forgotten about the shattered mug. Perhaps that was what the guys on the patio were looking at. Maybe they had remained unaware that anything happened.

Not likely.

"I tripped," I said.

"You tripped, huh?" Alik drummed his fingertips on the table. "Do you think this is a game?"

"A game? What?"

"You have to remain invisible, Jack. You may not understand the power that Ivanov wields, but I do. He has puppets everywhere in Moscow. If he finds out you are here, this place will be crawling with his men. We'll both hang. So until Frank can get us out of here, you need to stay out of trouble."

"Jesus Christ," I said. "I got knocked over by someone hurrying out of here. That's all. I didn't start anything. Didn't say anything. Got an elbow to my side and my face planted into the floor. My mug shattered. That's why I'm bleeding."

He slid a napkin across the table. "OK, well, just consider that other stuff a reminder."

"Trust me, man. I just want to go home. The sooner that happens, the better. As nice as this place is, my heart skips a beat every time that door opens."

Alik nodded as though he felt the same.

Then we both turned as the door whipped open again.

## 3

Four men I had never seen entered the cafe. A fifth guy followed. I recognized him. He'd been in there a few minutes ago.

"Shit," I said.

"What?" Alik said.

"That's the guy that knocked me over."

Alik nodded. Said nothing. He narrowed his eyes and studied the guys.

"And roughed up Esau," I said.

"These guys are new in town," Alik said. "Some of the locals said they're trouble. Criminals."

"And they want something with Esau."

The five men stood near the door. They were carbon copies of each other. Their gazes swept across the room. Sizing up the place. All around, old guys rose, dropped cash on the tables, and left. They stared at the floor as they squeezed past the group at the exit.

I wondered what the hell was going on.

Alik shot me a look as though to say leave it alone.

And I did.

At least, I tried.

The men gathered around the table nearest the counter. They were loud. Tossed leftover plates at the display case like discs. One splintered the glass, leaving a crack that ran top to bottom. They taunted Isadora, too. I wasn't sure what they said, but heard Esau's name mentioned a time or two.

Isadora looked frightened. She had no way out. Head for the front or back door, and they'd cut her off. Did Esau keep a weapon behind the counter? Hopefully she was smart enough to leave it alone if he did. Nothing good would come from pulling a gun on this group.

I rose, drawing the attention of the men. They watched me cross the room toward the counter. I kept a row of tables between me and them. No point in giving them an easy shot.

On the wall behind Isadora, a stainless steel paper towel dispenser hung. I positioned myself so I could use it like a mirror. Gave me a view of the group seated nearby.

She forced a smile. She rubbed her palms and pulled on her fingers one at time. There was fear behind her eyes. She knew why the men were here, and it scared her.

"Everything OK?" I asked her.

She nodded, tight and terse. Her lips thinned. I couldn't tell if she was trying to comfort me, or looking for me to do so for her.

"How about another cup of coffee?" I said.

She turned and grabbed a mug. Filled it. Dropped a cube of sugar and splashed some milk.

Behind me, the guy who'd slammed into me earlier rose.

The smug smile plastered on his face indicated he had no respect for me. He tapped one of the others on the shoulder and jutted his chin at me, as if to say, watch what I do to this guy next.

Isadora set the mug on the counter. Her gaze traveled to my left. I grabbed the handle. My knuckle pressed against the hot ceramic. I studied the makeshift mirror, waiting until the guy was two feet behind me. He stopped. I turned, mug outstretched, ready to coat him with piping hot coffee.

The guy's wide smile revealed yellow stained teeth. His breath stunk of moldy cheese. He had a five-day-old beard. Half of it white. The hair on his head was solid black.

"We got a problem here?" I said.

He lifted his arms and shrugged. Kept smiling. His hot breath continued its assault on my face. A few seconds later, he took a half step back, turning his shoulders parallel with the door, giving me the out to avoid contact as I passed on my way back to the table.

Why take that, though?

I opted to pay him back for bowling through me earlier. I secured the mug in both hands and slammed my right shoulder into the guy's torso. Probably didn't hurt him. Sent a wave of pain through my ribs though.

The guy stumbled back a couple steps and laughed. "That all you got, you stupid American?"

I headed for the table, and didn't look back. Alik sat there, shaking his head. Something soft hit me and fell to the floor with barely a thud. Alik glanced down at the crumpled up napkin, then up at me.

"What part of stay invisible don't you get?" he said. "You are supposed to be a ghost. Stay out of this."

I positioned myself to keep an eye on the five men. Their voices rose. The ones facing me stared. The ones seated with their backs to me tossed glances over their shoulders. I managed to catch the name of the guy who knocked me down earlier. Michael. He nodded when one in his group said it. Their actions earlier and now indicated that they hadn't come here for me, but I'd become a part of their plans. A hindrance, perhaps. Maybe a focal point.

I looked at Alik. "Is that what your gut is telling you? Ignore what's going on in here?"

He said nothing. Wouldn't make eye contact. Sat there with his arms crossed, shaking his head.

"You know damn well these guys are about to shake that old man down. That kind of activity never stops, man. And what do you think is going to happen after? We live here now. This is gonna trickle down to us."

"You don't care about that."

"Maybe I don't. Truth is, I'd rather avoid that happening at all. I'd be content to get on a plane and head back to New York right now. But that ain't happening. This is."

"Jack, you ever spent time with, what would you call them, country folk or rednecks or farming type people?"

"Sure."

"OK, these people in this town have that kind of mindset. So, you see, what they consider criminals might not be what we think of. Corruption runs wild in this country. These men could be part of the government. They might be here working on the side, but I can assure you, get in their way and they could make life hell for us."

I leaned to the side and watched the men. Could they be government agents or some kind of law enforcement? Sure.

Hell, most people couldn't spot the guys doing the dirty work back in the States. But there was something missing. Government agent types wouldn't be so brazenly stupid in public. They'd do their dirty work behind the scenes. Intimidation worked. But these guys were using it overtly.

"You know that's not the case," I said. "These guys are thugs. Maybe organized, but thugs all the same."

"Sometimes, there isn't much of a difference between guys like us, and guys like them."

Three of the men got up and left. Including Michael, the guy who'd planted me on the floor earlier. Their absence helped ease the tension in the cafe. We were on even ground. Sort of. I presumed the men were armed, but hadn't confirmed it.

"Think we should go?" Alik said.

"Hell no," I said.

"Seems like they're leaving."

"Still two here. I'm not getting up until they're gone."

"What if they stay all night?"

"Then so do we."

"Dammit, Jack."

The shadows on the floor tightened as the sun rose above the windows. I got up once. Went to the counter and dropped off my plate. The men at the table ignored me.

A short while later, the three men returned. The table was once again bustling with activity.

And Isadora had their full attention.

# 4

THEY TOOK TURNS GOING TO THE COUNTER, SLAPPING THE stainless steel, and shouting at Isadora. Alik translated, but with all the voices and laughter and noise, he had trouble delivering a full transcript. He fell behind and stuck to pointing out key words.

*Where's Esau?*

*Money.*

*Where's the damn money?*

*Where's he hiding it?*

The exchange painted a picture of the man who'd only shown kindness. He'd found himself in trouble with these guys over a debt. For what, though? Seemed Esau had everything he needed here. Of course, it didn't always work that way. Demons are excellent at hiding.

"These guys are the thugs," Alik said. "What if the man or whoever they work for is part owner in the cafe? They're here to collect his cut."

"Or maybe they're trying to collect a tax," I said. "They're collectors for the local mob."

Alik shrugged. "Doesn't look like any of our business."

"Are you fucking kidding me? Do you really lack the balls to stand up and defend her?"

"No. What I lack is the ability to disobey a direct order."

"Yeah, well, that's my specialty."

I swept the table for the thin serrated knife. It wasn't there. I'd left it at the counter. The only weapon I had was my fists. In a lot of cases that would be enough. But in my current condition, not so much.

Isadora looked my way. Must've noticed I was about to do something by the way I sat, poised to attack. She shook her head, a slight movement once to each side. She didn't have to say anything. I saw the pleading in her eyes. She didn't want to be responsible for me getting beat down for helping. At the same time she needed my help before the men got out of control.

One of the men rose from the table. He walked to the front door and blocked it. The other four assaulted the counter together and shouted at Isadora from the other side of it. She served it back to them.

Alik said, "He'll go see him later."

"What?" I said.

"That's what she's telling them. Esau will go see him later."

"Who is him?"

"How should I know?"

Michael reached across the counter and grabbed a tendril of Isadora's hair. He yanked her forward, planting her face into the top of the display case. She cried out in pain. He pulled her head up. Blood trickled from her nose.

Alik swatted at me as I rose. He missed. I stormed across the room, ignoring the burning in my ribs.

One guy turned to intercept me, but lost his balance as I dodged his advance. A touch was all it took to redirect him into one of his associates. They collided and stumbled over a chair.

A third man managed to get in between me and Michael. He put his hand on my left shoulder. I reached across with my right. Grabbed his wrist. Torqued his arm back at an unnatural angle. He dropped to his knees and I drove my foot into his gut.

I looked up and saw Michael facing me. He let go of Isadora's hair and lunged forward, swinging his fist in my direction. I couldn't avoid the blow, but managed to slide enough to the right to catch it on my ear. I countered with a right hook to his side. He rose up and bowed out in the other direction. I drew my arm back to deliver the knockout punch. Someone intercepted it. Turned me around. My knees were chopped at the side and I hit the ground.

Two bodies crashed into the display case. Alik must've flown across the room and plowed into the guy who'd taken me down.

I lunged into someone's knees. Something snapped as he went sideways. Ended up taking down two guys.

Alik and I could win five against two in some situations. This wasn't one of them. I was still too weak and fatigued, and Michael had re-injured my ribs earlier. On top of that, these men seemed trained. Our best hope was to extend the fight until the fear of help arriving settled in.

It seemed as though there was no chance of that happening.

I found myself pulled up, then pinned against the counter by two men. Michael stood in front of me. Blood poured from his split lip. He ran his tongue over the wound, then spat crimson tinted saliva at me. I struggled against the arms that pinned me, but got nowhere.

The other two guys held Alik to the ground. They hiked his arms behind his back and dragged him across the room.

Behind the counter, Isadora shouted. "Leave them alone. They've got nothing to do with this."

The guy in front of me said, "Then they should have kept their dumb American noses out of this."

I laughed. Hurt like hell to do so.

"What's so funny?" the guy said.

"He's Russian, you dumbass."

Michael drew his hand up high across his chest like he was going to backhand me.

Esau emerged from the stairwell, past his office. "What is going on here? Leave these men alone."

All five men looked at the old guy. They released Alik. Michael took a couple steps back, nodded at the two men holding me. They released my arms. I helped Alik to his feet. Isadora went to her uncle. Alik and I positioned ourselves between them and the five men.

One of the men left the cafe. The bells jingled as the door opened and fell shut. Ragged breathing filled the room. Angry stares flitted between us.

Why had the guys halted their attack? They had us dead to rights. Could have taken us outside and thrown us over the railing onto the rocky shore. Could've dragged us out of the cafe, thrown us in the trunk of their car, taken us out of town and executed us. But they stopped when Esau showed up. He was important. We were a distraction.

The door opened again. The guy who'd left stepped in. A

sixth man followed him. He looked different from the others. Less Greek. He dressed better, too, clad in a dark suit and expensive shoes. Where they looked like men who lived to fight and shake down their boss's customers, this guy was cool and calculated. He didn't need to be in a group to handle himself, yet he used the power of the men to do his will. But he wasn't the boss. The boss wouldn't show his face in such a public place during an event like this. I figured this guy only stepped in when necessary.

And we had made it so.

He walked past his men and stopped in front of me. He stood an inch taller, but wasn't as wide in the shoulders. His light-brown beard was trimmed to maybe a quarter of an inch. He stood there for a moment, staring me down. Then he stepped to the side and continued on. I looked back. Saw him thump Esau in the chest.

"Let's go." He looked back at his men and gave them a circling gesture with his finger. They retreated to the front door, effectively barricading it from ingress and egress, as Esau and the guy disappeared into the office.

Isadora retreated behind the counter for a second, then came over to me. She offered me a wet towel. I wiped my face with it. Wasn't sure if the blood it removed belonged to me.

Tension filled the cafe. It smelled of coffee, pastry, and sweat. The rumbling waves and persistent wind howled through the room. Three of the men lifted their shirts and placed their hands on hidden weapons. Why hadn't they used them? Not even for a threat? Someone had told them not to, no matter the situation. I doubted they had expected the kind of resistance they encountered.

Isadora returned to the busy side of the counter. She paced on a five-foot tract, her gaze never wavering from the wall that separated her from her uncle.

I strained to listen in on the conversation in the office. Heard nothing. Wouldn't have mattered if I did since they likely spoke in Greek.

Fifteen minutes passed. The men at the door took turns stepping out. Each time the door opened, I caught the scent of seared tobacco.

When the guy finally left the office, he took a path that led right through me. His hard soles slapped the tile, slowly and deliberately. He slipped his hands inside his pockets. Stopped three feet from me. His gaze worked from my feet to my eyes.

There was no sign of fear in the guy. He could handle himself, and he knew it. Worse, he knew that I knew it. He had a background that paralleled mine in some way. He was more than a common criminal. He had military and government training and experience.

He stared at me as though he considered how to handle me. If he stepped to the side, I won. That was unacceptable.

Same went for me. I wasn't about to give the guy ground. But adrenaline had worn off. My ribs hurt like hell. Knuckles felt swollen. I ached in spots where I'd been punched and kicked.

Esau stepped out of his office. He held a bloodstained cloth to his nose. He wiped his face, then tucked the cloth in his pocket. He walked like a man with a vertebra out of place. Back arched, shoulders held back, feet shuffling along the floor. He pushed past the guy in front of me.

"Enough, Chris," he said to the guy. "Get out. You and all your bastards."

Chris turned his head toward the old man, but kept looking at me. "Twelve hours, Esau. That's all he's giving you."

# 5

THE GUYS AT THE DOOR FILED OUT, ONE AT A TIME. THEY LOOKED left and turned right and slipped out of view. Chris was the last to leave. He stopped in the open doorway and looked back. His gaze traveled slowly across the room until it met mine. No words were exchanged, but his intent was clear. Intimidation. He stared me down as though he were saying *I'll be back to deal with you later.*

He said something in Greek, and followed it up with a hand gesture, then let the door fall shut.

Esau charged forward. He threw his weight into the door to expedite its closing. The lock engaged with a thud.

"What'd he say?" I said to Alik.

Alik shrugged. "It didn't make sense to me. Maybe some kind of code that only Esau would understand?"

Isadora went to her uncle and wrapped her arms around his neck. She choked back sobs. He patted her back and soothed her in muffled tones.

"I'm sorry," he said to us. "Sorry that you two got mixed up in that. It is not what it looked like."

Isadora stared at the floor.

"Then what is it?" I said.

Esau sighed as he pulled away from his niece. He gestured for her to sit down. She twisted a seat until it faced the window and collapsed into it.

"It is something that goes back a long ways," he said. "And it doesn't concern you. From now on, if you see those men, you get up and you leave. They are not to be messed with. Understand?"

"Understand?" I said. "I'm not your damn kid, Esau. You can't brush me off like that."

"How about I kick you two out, then? Huh?" Esau's cheeks burned red. "What if I notify someone in the government that you two are hiding out here? What happens then?"

"You threatening us?" Alik said.

Isadora rose and placed herself between us and her uncle. "No, he's not. He's just angry. Frustrated. He's taking it out on you two when he should be thinking about other things. Isn't that right, Uncle?"

Esau assumed the posture of a defeated man. "Yes, I'm just trying to do the right thing here. Please, avoid those men." He walked up to Isadora and touched his hand to her elbow. He led her past us without either of them making eye contact. Esau ushered his niece into his office and shut the door.

The air inside the cafe went still. The sound of the waves diminished. The front, back, office, and stairwell doors were closed. The fan switched off. Isadora's perfume lingered, mixing with sweat and stale coffee and pastries.

"Let's go upstairs," Alik said.

As we made our way to the stairs, Esau emerged from his office. He stopped, looked at us, then continued to the terrace door. He flipped the lock and headed back.

"We'll reopen around five. Please leave us alone until then."

## 6

I washed up, changed into clean shorts and a white t-shirt. Made my way into the living room and collapsed into a chair, facing the sea. Warm salt-laden air washed over me. I placed a bag of ice against my ribs and held it in place with my arm. The contrast between where the bag pressed into my flesh and the rest of my body was like black and white.

Alik was standing in the kitchen, holding a glass tumbler filled with clear liquid. He looked over, nodded, grabbed another glass. He picked up a bottle that had a red, white and blue label and filled the tumbler with ouzo.

"A little early, don't you think?" I said.

"It'll help dull the pain," he said. "Besides, we don't have to finish off the whole bottle."

"Might keep us out of trouble if we did."

Alik laughed, lowering himself onto the couch, a green fabric thing that looked like it belonged in the seventies.

He said, "Knowing you, we'd end up deported."

I said, "Then my life can go back to normal."

"I thought this was normal for you? Getting caught up in other people's problems. Getting your ass kicked."

"Whatever." I took a sip of the ouzo, wincing as the liquor slid down my parched throat. It continued on. The warmth in my stomach radiated outward. "If I wasn't in such bad shape none of those guys would've stood a chance."

"Is that so?" Alik leaned back with both arms spread over the back of the couch. "What about that sixth man?"

"You spotted that too, huh?"

He nodded.

"I don't know what to think of him," I said. "Different from the others, for sure. You see how they all tightened up when he came in?"

Alik nodded, remained quiet.

"And he didn't show any fear," I said. "Obviously he's from somewhere else. The way he acted tells me his background is more aligned with ours."

"Could have been because he had five men with him. Three of whom were armed."

"How early did you catch that?"

"Before you did." He lifted his glass and tipped it toward me. "Before I jumped in to help you out."

"Thanks for that."

"Wasn't for your benefit, Jack. Something happens to you, I'm marked for death on three continents instead of just one."

We finished our drinks in silence. The wind died down. Sunlight poured through the windows. The heat of its rays warmed me, lulling me into a false sense of security. Eventually forcing me to doze off. I looked at my watch and determined I'd been out for half an hour when Alik woke me.

"What do you think he did?" Alik said.

I looked over at the man. His hair was wet and he'd changed clothes. His glass was filled to the rim again.

"Who?" I said.

"Esau," he said. "Who else?"

"I dunno. The president? Ivanov? Could be anyone, I guess."

"Smart ass," he said. "Anyway, I can't help but wonder what he did to bring this on himself."

"We really don't know the guy. Did your contact tell you anything about him?"

Alik shook his head. "All I got was a name and an address, along with a promise that the man would be on our side, so don't worry."

"Did you?"

"What?"

"Worry?"

"Of course I worried." Alik rose and walked to the window, blocking my view of the sea. "I had broken you out of Black Dolphin. I still don't know how I managed to get across the border and out of Russia with you. I thought we were both dead men at the crossing."

"I was too weak to move when they pried the lid off the pine casket. Damn eyelids didn't even clamp when the sun hit my face."

Alik laughed. "Morbid son of a bitch."

"Whatever."

"So what do you think he did?"

"Esau?"

Alik sighed and brought his glass to his forehead. "Yes, Esau."

"You heard them say money earlier, so I'm guessing he either owes a debt or a tax."

"Well, that's kind of what we figured earlier, right? I guess my question is over what?"

"Hard to tell when the guy won't tell us anything."

"He's a proud man."

"That's obvious."

He walked back to the couch, saying, "And I think we need to respect his wishes and stay out of this."

"Are you scared?"

Alik leaned forward, arms crossed over his knees, his drink supported by both hands. He stared down at the clear ouzo. Without looking up, he said, "Yes, Jack, I am. We don't know these men. We don't know what Esau did to get involved with them. We don't know their connections. Think for a moment. Follow the strands of the web as they work outward from the center here. What are some real possibilities here?"

"You complicate things too much," I said. "All I know is there's an old man down there who's getting bullied. We have the ability to stop it."

"You suffer from a curse, my friend." He jabbed a finger at me from six feet away. "And you would be better off doing what you are told instead of following your gut all the time."

"I spent years doing what I was told. Earned me a price on my head put there by the guy whose orders I followed."

Alik rose and shuffled to the kitchen. I stared out the window and watched a tanker pass in the distance. When Alik returned, he stood in front of me empty-handed, missing the third drink I expected him to be holding.

He said, "I'm leaving for a bit."

I said, "Where to?"

"Going to scrounge us up a few days' worth of food. I think it's best we stay up here in the apartment instead of venturing down to the cafe." He waved off my argument before I had the chance to state it. "At least until we know this mess has blown over. I can't help but think we — and by *we,* I mean *you* — made things worse for Esau and Isadora today."

He slid out of view. The door opened with a creak and shut with a soft thud. The lock made a clicking sound as he engaged it with his key. Alone in the apartment, I kept watch over the sea and mulled over his words. All along, Alik, Isadora, and Esau had all told me to stay out of it. What did I do? Jumped in headfirst. Was it due to a lack of action? Feeling like I needed to be involved in something to continue on? Or could I chalk this up to my stubborn nature? Sometimes it seemed that I'd rather use my head as a battering ram than for logical thinking.

I wanted to avoid the questions, not face them. The situation with Ivanov and in Black Dolphin had left me feeling susceptible for the first time since I was a kid. I felt as though I'd lost a bit of my edge. I didn't have the ability to back it up.

The scene in the cafe only helped to solidify those thoughts.

So perhaps Alik had a point. Whatever this was about, Esau had brought it upon himself. He didn't run or hide from the men. He didn't call the cops. He didn't accept my offer of help. And neither did Isadora. As young and beautiful and kind as she had been, she had a choice here too. And she chose to go it alone.

After several minutes debating the issue, I decided to back off. At least for a while.

I pushed a chair closer to the window. The wind picked up.

White caps approached in staggered lines from a hundred yards out. They pounded the rocky shore and it sounded like thunder. The spray rose into the air and rode on the wind and spattered my face. There was a coolness to the breeze that was lost inside the closed room.

So I left the apartment and went down the stairs en route to the terrace.

Isadora stopped when I stepped into the cafe. Her hair was pulled back. She held a broom at an angle, the bristles an inch off the floor. The chairs were perched upside down on the tables. Coffee percolated. The sign on the front door had been flipped and read open upside down.

"What's going on?" I asked her.

"Decided to remain closed for the day," she said.

"Worried those men are coming back?"

She smiled weakly. "No, I don't think we'll be seeing them for a few days at least."

"Then why shut down?"

"In a small town like this, word gets around quick. No one is going to come in tonight."

"Fear?"

"Shame." She drew the broom handle across her body. "No one stepped up to help. At least, no one local."

"They're smart."

"You're right, they are. You should have listened to Alik, Jack. To me and my uncle too. You want no part of this. It isn't even your battle. You owe my uncle nothing."

"Sure I do. He's put me up here despite possible ramifications. Besides, the men were getting rough with you. I had to intervene."

"No one laid a hand on me." She clutched the broom with

both hands and shrugged forward. "And I can take care of myself."

"They were close."

"I can take care of myself," she said again, a hint of force behind her words.

I threw my hands up in retreat. "Well, you don't have to worry. I decided that next time I see something going on, I'm just gonna walk away."

"I'm sorry." She set the broom against a table and crossed the room to me. Despite the long day, she looked and smelled as good as she had that morning. She rose onto the tips of her toes and wrapped her arms around my neck and pressed into me. Her breasts meshed with my chest. Her hips touched mine. Her soft lips grazed against my cheek and then my ear. Her words were hot against my skin. "Thank you. Your actions, though misguided, are appreciated."

She pulled away from me and retreated behind the counter.

I turned and stepped out onto the terrace. Her scent remained on me. Shades of red, orange and purple colored the horizon. I hadn't realized it was so late. The wind whipped in from the sea. It enveloped me, cooling my skin, taking a bite out of the humidity.

The terrace door opened. I turned, saw Isadora standing there. I resisted the urge to go to her, wanting instead for her to come to me.

She cleared her throat and spoke over the waves and wind. "I'm almost done in here. Can you lock up the terrace before you go back upstairs?"

"Can I walk you home?"

Her gaze lifted. She sighed. "Always the good Samaritan?"

I crossed the terrace and stopped a few feet short of where I wanted. "I'd feel better after all that happened today."

She turned toward the cafe's dining room. I stepped in front of the shifting door and followed close behind.

"Fine," she said. "But we had better go so you aren't walking the mean streets of Palaiochora alone in the dark."

## 7

THE BUILDINGS ON EITHER SIDE OF THE STREET WERE TWO OR three stories, sandstone and white. The odd alley ran between them, allowing slices of orange sunlight to knife across the road. When we walked through those spots, Isadora's hair shone like golden thread. A few older people were out, sitting on benches, the hum of their chatter filling the street. The air was cool, yet humid, and smelled of searing meat.

Isadora said she lived with Esau, about two miles from the cafe. We didn't speak the first few minutes. Then she told me a little about her upbringing. I offered her a little about mine. Halfway to her uncle's house, she recounted the story of how she'd ended up in town.

"When my mother's sister, Eleni, fell ill, my mother asked that I come to this town to help out with my aunt and uncle's business. Now, this was a big deal. I only had two more semesters at the university when Eleni became too sick to work in the cafe."

"And she ended up passing, right?"

"Yes."

"But not before you came?"

"Right."

"You gave it all up?"

She nodded. "That was four years ago."

"He couldn't get help in the time since?"

She shrugged. "Doesn't necessarily work like that."

"What do you mean?"

"It's a family business."

"But you were close to finishing school. Could've gone on to start your career."

Isadora stared at the ground and clutched her hands together behind her back. "My sister took my place."

"How do you mean?"

"My parents could only afford for one of us to be in school. Instead of her taking a year off to come here so I could go back and finish, my parents sent her to university."

"Why didn't she come help at the cafe?"

"I already knew how to run the place."

"Come on," I said. "It's not rocket science."

"No, it's not. But dealing with my uncle is another story. And my sister is not me. She doesn't have the same kind of, what would you say, work ethic. I think if she had come here, she would have ruined the business. Especially considering Uncle Esau's state of mind since my aunt passed. Do not get me wrong. It has improved. But he always seems distracted, like he's thinking of her non-stop. It really breaks my heart."

"So that's it? You give up your future, and you're OK with it?"

"Who said I'm OK? I accept it. And I know that my little

sister will be done with school soon, and I'll be able to return. I'm not giving up on myself. Haven't you ever cared for someone so much you gave up things that meant the world to you?"

I said nothing.

Her hands fell to her side, her right brushing my left. She glanced over. "You have a habit of interjecting your opinion on everything, don't you?"

"Not everything," I said. "I tend to avoid certain topics."

"Yeah, like what?"

I shrugged. "Women's water polo, for one."

She smiled at the remark and nudged me with her elbow.

"I'm just asking questions," I said. "I can stop."

"I don't mind, I guess." She came to a halt. "Why are you staring at me like that?"

"You remind me of someone back home."

"A special someone?"

"At times."

"What's she like?"

"Strong willed and pig headed. A lot like you, actually."

Isadora shoved me, her hands pressing into my ribs. I tried to mask the pain. Didn't work.

"You're not healed yet, are you?" Her hands remained, but they opened and gently pressed into my chest.

"Getting there. Didn't help they managed to connect a few times where the ribs had been broken."

She regarded me in the fading light. "So you've heard a little about me. Who are you, Jack?"

"I'm just a pawn."

"For?"

"The highest bidder."

"Sounds intriguing."

"It is. You should read the book when it comes out."

"Everyone's got their secrets," she said.

"Guess so," I said. "What's yours?"

"I told you mine. I still hold out hope for a better future even though the odds are stacked against me."

"A woman like you, the odds will always be in your favor."

She smiled as her hands trailed down my arms until her left hand latched onto my right. She turned and tugged me forward. We covered the last quarter mile in silence. By the time we reached the house, the sky was dark and the only illumination came from porch lights. The sound of the sea was faint. The wind rustled through trees and bushes. It whipped her hair and it brushed against my cheek a couple times.

"The lavender," I said.

"What about it?" she said.

"It's in your hair."

She grabbed several strands and held them to her nose. "An oil I rub in."

"All day long I thought it was your perfume."

"All day, huh?" she smiled.

I said nothing.

"Maybe when you're feeling better, I can get a day off and show you the island."

"I don't know. The more you're with me, the more you might uncover some more secrets."

"Don't worry, I'm good at withholding information, Jack." Her smile lingered as she jutted her chin toward a white house. Her eyes flicked in that direction, then back at me. "That's my stop."

I walked her to the door and waited while she unlocked and opened it.

"Should I invite you in?" she asked.

"Is that you, Isa?" Esau called from another room.

"Yes, Uncle," she said over her shoulder.

"Who are you talking to?" Esau said.

"I swear he's got sonic hearing," she whispered.

I took a few steps back. "You should get inside."

"It's OK if you want to come in."

Esau had been good to Alik and me. He'd housed and fed us, and it didn't matter why we needed the help. I appreciated that he stuck out his neck for us, two men he had never met. After what had happened today, it felt like imposing if I remained any longer.

"I'll see you tomorrow," I said, turning away.

It was pitch black out. The sun was gone. The moon hadn't risen. I could barely see the ground. If not for the random house light, I might not have found my way back to the town and the cafe.

The day's events played over in my head. I watched them like a movie, without interjecting thought or opinion into scenes. I thought about the corners of the cafe, the street just beyond the window. Looked for other faces I didn't recognize. If there were any, I'd blocked them out. I winced at every blow. Didn't help that I felt the pain in my side with every step I took. I considered myself fortunate that my lung hadn't collapsed again. All the more reason to be careful. I had to accept that I wasn't myself. I couldn't dish out punishment like normal. I didn't recover from my injuries the same way. It was harder to work through them.

"God, am I getting old?" I muttered.

The wind mocked me with a gust that sounded like a long drawn out *yes*. I chose not to listen.

The first streetlight loomed in the distance, an orange halo in the darkness. The light wash grew as I drew nearer, illuminating the street, grass, bushes. A few minutes later the shadows were confined to the alleyways. Every sound echoed down the corridor of two- and three-story buildings, all orange in the electric haze. Even my own footsteps ratcheted into a sound akin to downrange automatic gunfire.

Three blocks from the cafe the sound was interrupted. Someone clearing their throat. Could have been my mind transmuting the sound of the waves. But when it was followed by a foot slapping the ground, my gut and chest tightened.

I shifted my eyes. Saw nothing. Moved my head. Still saw nothing. I stopped and leaned against the wall, pretending to search my pockets for a phone or a cigarette. I casually looked back in the direction I'd come from. Shadows played across the empty street.

I considered that my mind was playing tricks on me. The action I'd seen today was the first I'd encountered in over six weeks. I wasn't used to the rush of adrenaline and the drive to fight. My system needed the counteraction. It wanted me to take flight. So my brain created this scenario, taking a simple noise and exaggerating it into a threat.

With the cafe close, I quickened my pace. I heard nothing other than the sounds of my steps and my heart whooshing in my ears.

I approached the final alley too quickly. Felt it as I stepped into the darkness. They were all around me. Had to be the guys from earlier. They'd seen me leave the cafe with Isadora and had lain in wait for an hour for this very moment.

I stopped in the middle, spun in place, threw my hands into a defensive position.

"Come on you bastards," I said to the darkness. "Come get me."

No one did.

My eyes adjusted to the shadows. I saw the dumpster and grease trap. A couple trash cans. A cat perched on top of one.

No assailants.

But that's because they hit me from behind.

## 8

THE GUY DID IT RIGHT. HE GOT AN ARM AROUND MY NECK, choking off my air supply. He pulled one arm behind my back, twisted and torqued, forcing me to turn sideways to relieve the pain. I swung my free arm, but the awkward angle meant even the blows that connected were too weak to inflict anything other than an itch. And with every passing second, my lungs screamed louder and my vision closed tighter and my brain grew lighter.

Then he let go, shoved with his hands, stuck a foot out in front of me. My face hit the ground before I managed to break my fall. The concrete grated against my right cheek. The ground stunk like old grease and trash. The wind blew cigarette butts toward me.

Why had he released me? He couldn't control what I did now. There would be a fight.

I rolled over, expecting to see three to five armed men

staring back at me. To my surprise, one guy stood there. And he was unarmed.

"Alik? The hell you doing?"

"What am I doing? I should be asking you the same. What were you thinking going out after what happened today?"

"I took a walk. What's the big deal?"

"A walk? You think I'm stupid. I followed you and her all the way to Esau's house."

"You were there the whole time?"

Alik stepped forward and offered his hand. I took it, and he pulled me up.

"When are you going to accept that you are not up for this, Jack? You are not ready. You are not the guy you were two months ago."

Alik's words echoed my own thoughts at that moment. How had I missed him? Four miles he tailed me, and I didn't come close to realizing someone was there until the end. And even then my instincts were wrong. I relied on guesswork and nearly paid the price. I had no idea which way he had come from. My stinging cheek could've been a bullet to my head.

I said, "I didn't feel comfortable watching her leave alone after what happened today."

Alike intertwined his fingers and flexed them. "I understand, Jack. I do. I feel the same way as you."

"You don't act like it."

"We have been through this, my friend. The job dictates everything. I do not allow my personal feelings to interfere."

"It's not personal," I said. "It's just who I am."

"You're going to tell me you haven't developed some feelings for this woman?"

I shrugged. It was something I'd shuffled to the recesses of my mind.

Alik laughed. "First of all, she is too young for you."

"Saying I'm old?"

He gestured at my hunched posture. "You tell me."

"I'm beat up a bit, and you just knocked me to the ground."

"Exactly."

"Whatever." I headed toward the building's side door.

Alik caught up and stuck his key in the lock. "She's attractive. I'll give you that."

I said nothing.

"But still too young for you."

I pushed the door open and stepped into the dark corridor. Felt my way along the wall until I reached the stairwell. I counted the twelve steps up, then kept my hand on the wall until I reached the apartment door. Alik followed behind, whistling a tune I hadn't heard before. Figured it was a Russian song. He walked around me. His keys jingled as he inserted the right one into the lock.

A steady stream of wind blew through the open window. Pages of a magazine on the coffee table flapped. Alik flipped on the light. We both scanned the room, looking for anything out of place, then he went to the kitchen. Early on we had agreed to keep certain items in specific locations. Then if anything had been moved, we would know someone else had been inside.

Everything remained where we had left it.

"Hungry?" Alik said.

"Starving," I said.

"Bet so. You took two beatings today."

"I wasn't sure how many of you were behind me. That's the only reason you weren't the one who landed on your face."

"Keep telling yourself that, my friend."

"Another month and you can take a shot at the championship."

Alik grabbed a couple spice bottles, looked back, smiled. "Are you really that confident, or do you just try to make people think you are?"

"Is there a difference? I mean, it's all mind games anyhow. Training and experience gives me a leg up on most people. But beyond that, it's what I exude that makes the difference. Take that guy I was in the cell with in Black Dolphin."

He unwrapped some ground lamb and placed it in a bowl. "Yeah, he was a nasty man. No doubt why they stuck you with him."

"Right. Any other time, the crimes he committed, that guy is in isolation the rest of his life. They put me in there so the guy could break me until he killed me."

"But you took him down. How? Don't get me wrong. I know you can fight. But you should not have won that battle."

"And that's exactly what he thought. So when I didn't back down, when I went on the offensive, he didn't know how to react. His whole life, I bet no one ever picked a fight with the guy, except maybe his dad. And I'm not sure about that."

"Well, no matter now I suppose. You won't go back there."

"No," I said. "I figure if Ivanov gets his hands on me again, I'm a dead man."

Alik dumped the meat into the frying pan. Smoke rose as the lamb sizzled in a layer of olive oil. The wind wrapped the smell of meat and seasonings around me, making my mouth water.

"Me, too," Alik said. "And that is why we have to keep our heads down until whenever Skinner reaches out for us."

"I know, I know." I leaned back and closed my eyes. "I don't need another damn lecture."

Alik laughed. I heard a couple bottles clink together, then thump on the counter. Caps were twisted and carbonation hissed. "How about a beer then?"

"Sounds good to me."

We drank a couple beers, ate dinner, and talked about the differences growing up in Russia and the States. The beer helped numb my ribs and other wounds. The talk helped lull me into a relaxed state. And within a couple hours, I was asleep.

## 9

I WOKE EARLY THE NEXT MORNING TO THE SOUND OF MY curtains flapping in the wind. The smells of breakfast wafted into the room. It felt comfortable in the apartment, but I wanted to get out for a while. I started a pot of coffee and left before it finished.

Downstairs, forks clanked against plates and soft chatter filled the cafe. Only one table was occupied. The couple sitting there ran the florist shop two doors down. The cafe smelled of butter and eggs and meat and coffee. Isadora stood behind the counter, dressed similar to every other day, except a white blouse covered her t-shirt. She saw me, smiled, turned away. I took it as a sign she didn't want me in there. She spun back toward me with a mug.

"Take this," she said. "I'll fix you some breakfast. Have it ready in a few."

I grabbed the mug and headed out to the empty terrace. The

sea reflected the morning sky in such a way it was impossible to determine where the sky ended and the water began.

I leaned over the railing and focused on the shimmering horizon. The smell of the grill filtered out and mingled with the salt air. Seagulls sang and rode wind currents a hundred feet up. Out there was where I felt most comfortable. The small town should have left me feeling confined. But when I looked at the sea, all that melted away.

A few minutes later, Isadora came out with a plate of eggs covered with lamb meat. The dish had grown on me over the past few weeks.

"Quiet here today," I said.

She nodded and set the plate down at the table closest to where I stood.

"Think you'll do any business this morning?" I said.

She shrugged. "Some days we don't do much. It's OK."

"What do you do when that happens?"

"Read. Watch people on the street. Come out here and stare at the sea. That's about it, I guess." She smiled and gestured to the food. "Now sit down and eat before it gets cold."

I enjoyed the tranquility of the deserted patio while eating. But it felt off. I'd grown used to the banter of the old men. The gossip of the old ladies. The hurried shopkeepers taking a few moments to relax in the presence of others. The random tourists who remark about the serene town and the simple beauty of the sea.

I started to blame myself for the place being empty. Maybe if I hadn't intervened in what had happened yesterday, customers would be filling the cafe. Instead, they'd heard about the guy from the States opening his big mouth and starting something with the shady guys who'd been hanging around town.

*Typical, Jack.*

But I knew the early hour had something to do with it. I hoped, at least. It wasn't yet eight, and I was rarely down there that early. I finished my food, pushed the plate away, and leaned back in the chair, easing into the wrought iron back to minimize pain to my ribs. With my eyes closed, the sounds and smells lulled me into a meditative state. It wasn't quite sleep, as I remained aware of my surroundings.

The string of bells hanging from the door jingled inside the cafe. Several feet pounded the tile floor, echoed off the walls and ceiling, growing louder.

The morning rush.

Isadora gasped.

Plates fell to the floor and shattered. Glass fragments scattered like diamonds that had fallen from the sky.

A man said something in Greek. He didn't yell, but his tone was forceful. Isadora shouted at him.

Then the chaos began.

I jumped from my chair and headed to the open door. Saw five guys crowding the middle of the cafe. They were dressed the same as yesterday. Casual, dark clothes. All had their backs or sides to me. At least four had their hands wrapped around weapons.

Michael, the asshole who'd knocked me to the ground the day before, lunged over the counter. Isadora turned and ducked. Not fast enough, though. The guy grabbed a handful of her dark hair. She screamed and dug her nails into the flesh of his arms. He pressed a foot into the display case and pushed back from the counter. The force of the move yanked Isadora up and toward him.

I burst through the opening and kicked the first guy I saw in the back. He bowed forward and fell to his knees with a grunt. Two other men turned toward me.

I struck the first with a knifing jab that hit him in the soft spot of his neck, below the Adam's apple and above the tip of his sternum. His shoulders hunched up and his chin fell to his chest. I took a step to my right, then kicked his left knee on the side, buckling it. The guy went down hard on his side.

Michael had let go of Isadora's hair and now held her by the ankles. He yanked repeatedly. She clutched the far side of the counter. Her fingertips turned white. Another guy joined Michael and they tugged and pulled her free. She fell to the floor, managing to create a cushion for her face with her forearm. She cried out as it took the brunt of the fall.

Another guy came at me, throwing a wide right hook. I stepped in and blocked it with my left. Hefted my right elbow up, then drove it down on the bridge of his nose. His head snapped back. Blood sprayed in all directions. I slammed my fist into his gut. He bent forward. I grabbed the back of his head and drove my knee into his face, then discarded him to the side.

No one stood between Isadora and me. I darted toward her.

And then I was upended. Spent a second in the air, then landed on my side. Fortunately, it was the left side. Unfortunately, pain radiated out from my hip and my leg felt numb.

I didn't have long to work out what had happened. Hands wrapped around my upper arms and yanked me off the floor. They shoved me against the display case, slamming my forehead into it hard enough to crack the glass. And judging by the trail of blood that slid down the case, my forehead had cracked, too.

"What is going on in here?"

I forced my head to the side and saw Esau standing outside

his office, armed with a pistol. He extended the weapon at the men surrounding me. They let go. I heard them step back a few feet. I reached up for the counter and straightened my back. Esau nodded at me. I turned around, toward the front of the cafe, and saw five men lined up like scrawny offensive linemen with Michael in the middle. I'd left visible wounds on two of them. A third stood like I'd broken one or two of his ribs. Their quarterback, Chris, who had been absent until now, stood behind them. I saw Isadora through the line of thugs. Hair covered half her face. Chris held his pistol to her exposed temple.

"Put it away, old man," he said.

"Let my niece go," Esau said.

The guy cocked the hammer and pressed the muzzle against Isadora's temple. "Do it."

Esau trembled as he lowered his weapon.

"Good," the guy said. "Now, do you have what we talked about?"

Esau shook his head. "Like I told you yesterday, it's gone."

He clicked his tongue a couple times, admonishing Esau. "I'm afraid I'm going to have to take some collateral then until you've got it."

"What are you doing?" Isadora said.

The guy wrapped his arm over her breasts and dragged her toward the door. One of the five linemen broke away and opened it. Michael pulled his weapon and kept it aimed at the floor.

"Let her go." I lunged forward.

Three men rushed to meet me.

I aimed for the biggest and drove my foot into his crotch. Then I connected with the guy on the right with a wide hook.

But I couldn't reach the third in time. He dove into me. We crashed into the display case and then fell to the floor. My injured ribs took the brunt of the fall.

The two other guys regained composure, and a few seconds later, the three of them pinned me against the counter. Michael stepped forward and backhanded me twice. Then he took a few steps back and cocked his arm. He was going to take a running start on this blow.

"Let's get out of here," the guy at the door yelled.

Michael shook his head. "Next time, there won't be a time crunch."

They let go of me. I tried to run after them, but took a couple steps and collapsed to the floor where I watched them exit to the sidewalk where a late-model white sedan had pulled up. They shoved Isadora into the back. The rest got in and the vehicle drove out of sight.

# 10

---

ALIK ARRIVED THIRTY SECONDS LATER, NEARLY KNOCKING THE front door off its hinges. His breathing was fast and deep and ragged, as though he'd sprinted from a couple blocks away. He looked at Esau, me, then the street.

"They took Isadora," he said as though we hadn't witnessed it. A few breaths later, he added, "Jack, what the hell happened?"

I rolled over and held out my arm. Alik came over, helped me to my feet.

"Are you OK?"

I choked on a bit of blood, coughed, and spat on the floor. "More of the same. I'll be all right."

"What happened in here?"

I glanced at Esau. He stood stock still, staring at the pistol like it had let him down.

"The guys from yesterday came in and started busting up the place. I was outside when they arrived. Heard them and got up and saw them getting rough with Isadora, so I rushed in and took a few on. Didn't take long until I was overpowered, though. Esau came out, gun drawn. But they had her by then. Chris held a gun to her head, leaving us no choice. Maybe if I'd been armed, or in better shape, less beat up, it would've turned out different."

"I can't believe this," Esau muttered, eyes downcast, tears on his cheeks.

We both turned to him.

Alik said, "We need to call the police."

"No," Esau said, turning the pistol toward the Russian. "No police. Not now. Not ever. These men, they will kill her if there is the slightest hint we got the authorities involved."

"But it is obvious you know these men," Alik said. "You know their identities, correct?"

Esau looked away and said nothing.

"The authorities can use that information, locate them, and Isadora, and get her back home."

"Are you hard of hearing?" Esau said. "I said no police."

I stepped between the two men. "Esau, you're gonna have to level with us, then. Who are these guys, and what do they want with you and Isadora?"

He took a long moment to respond. "They went after her to get to me."

"We can see that," I said.

"They went after her," he said again, "to get to me."

I looked at Alik. He shrugged. We weren't the kind of guys used to gentle interrogations. But using force with the old man wasn't likely to do any good.

"I'm so ashamed." Esau slumped into a chair. He set his pistol on the table, then cupped his hands over his face. "How did I let this happen?"

"What did you let happen?" I said. "What are you ashamed about?"

Esau muttered something in Greek. I glanced at Alik, but he shrugged it off.

Alik said, "If you don't come clean with us, we'll have to call the authorities and get them involved."

Esau kept his hands over his face, shook his head.

I grabbed Alik and pulled him to the front of the cafe. The street stretched in both directions. Deserted. If anyone had witnessed the incident, they had left the scene. Couldn't blame them. Not in a town like this. Funny how it worked. In a big city, everyone would continue on as if nothing had happened, because they'd dulled themselves into ignoring everything around them. In this small town, there weren't enough numbers to provide that kind of anonymity. Yet they still kept to themselves.

"What do you think?" Alik said.

"No cops," I said.

He shook his head. "This is a mistake."

"We can handle this."

"We?"

"Yeah, you and I."

"You can't even defend yourself. All that recovery work is undone now. How do you think we will take these guys down?"

"I've handled more. Guys I knew were trained operatives."

"Aside from that," Alik said. "We don't even know where they are."

"True," I said, glancing at his reflection. "But I'm pretty sure Esau does."

"And he's a babbling fool right now."

"He knows what kind of men we are. I think if we offer our help to him, he'll open up."

"And if he doesn't?"

I glanced over my shoulder. Esau hadn't moved. "He'll lose his niece if he doesn't."

The old man lifted his chin off his chest and uncovered his face. "I know where they are."

## 11

Esau waited until evening. We drove his car to his house and went in together. Thick green carpet covered the floors wall to wall. The place looked like it had been furnished and decorated in the seventies and never updated. I wondered if the house had come furnished when he moved in, or were the furniture and fixtures representative of his tastes. It smelled like stale, burned coffee. Except when I walked past what must've been Isadora's room. I caught a whiff of her lavender fragrance.

Esau led us to the kitchen, which had a couple cabinets and linoleum floors and countertops made to look like marble. He pulled out a map of Crete and spread it on the table.

"This is where we are." Esau circled a spot in blue ink. "And the cafe is back here." Referring to the beaches, he added, "Over here is the touristy area. You're going to go past all that. Maybe fifteen miles. Right about here is an unmarked lane. Doesn't show on any of the maps, or on those GPS things, but it's there. You will know it by the wooden signpost that is so eroded you can't read what it once said. You turn there and go until it dead-ends. Say a quarter of a mile is how far it goes back. There's an old house there, the only one. That is where they stay when they come to town."

"How do you know this?" Alik said.

Esau tapped his finger on the spot and said nothing.

"Have you been there before?" Alik said.

Esau still said nothing.

"Have they taken you there before?"

Esau glanced up and nodded.

"What's going on here?" I said. "Tell us the truth."

Staring at the ceiling, the old man took a deep breath. "I need a drink. Get you guys something?"

Neither of us responded as Esau rose and stepped to the counter. He uncorked a bottle, poured his drink, returned with a glass in one hand, and a burning cigarette in the other.

The smoke swirled and spread. I resisted the urge to ask for one.

I said, "Back at the cafe you said this was all your fault and that they were using Isadora to get to you."

He sucked on the butt of the cigarette, said, "Yes."

"Care to elaborate?"

"I owe a debt."

"Can you pay it?"

"Not at the moment."

"Will you be able to pay it?"

He looked away. "I hope so."

"Say you can't," I said. "Say we rescue Isadora, and in doing so, we have to take out a couple of their men. What happens tomorrow when they find her gone? Find their guys dead?"

"They come back, I suppose."

"And this time they'll kill her."

His eyes glossed over and his lips trembled. The cigarette wavered in his shaking hand.

"If they haven't already." I balanced my chair on its rear legs. "Right?"

Esau nodded once. A tear slid down his cheek. I wondered if he feared Isadora was already dead.

Alik said, "How much money do you owe?"

Esau didn't answer the question. "You have to hurry. We're wasting time talking about this."

I looked at the darkened window. "We wasted time waiting until evening."

"No," he said. "They would have been watching the road. They would have known, and you would've walked into a trap."

"For some reason," I said, "I feel like I am now."

"Please, just get her. Bring her back here and I'll arrange for safe transport for the three of you. I'll deal with the men by myself tomorrow."

I glanced at Alik. He remained stoic. I couldn't read his face. It appeared he wanted to leave the decision up to me.

"OK," I said. "Your pistol, you bring it?"

Esau nodded, stood, lifted his shirt and then freed the handgun from his waistband. He set it on the table next to Alik. The Russian raised an eyebrow in my direction.

"Take it," I said.

"I've got this too." Esau turned and went to the kitchen. A drawer slid open. He rifled through papers. A few moments later he returned with a wooden sap. He slid it across the table to me.

It was old and weathered. Dented in a few spots. A hairline crack ran from the top down.

"A fine piece," I said.

"Was mine," Esau said. "During the war."

"Got a bit of use."

He smiled. "Back in the day, those six men would have found their skulls cracked and we would have tossed their brains into the sea."

I rose and grabbed the sap. Assuming a fighting stance, I balanced it in each hand. "I'll make sure you get it back, along with your niece."

Alik and I made our way to the front door. I slowed as we passed Isadora's room. The door was cracked, but the lights were off. An invisible wall of her smell was a welcome respite from the odor of the house.

"Wait," Esau called out. He went back into the kitchen, then returned with two small flashlights. "I don't know if that house has power or not."

I switched mine on and off. It wasn't powerful, but then again, I only needed to see a few feet ahead.

Alik took Esau's car keys and the driver's seat. Fine with me. My left hip still hurt, and the car was a manual shift. He started the engine and backed down the gravel driveway. The same one I'd walked Isadora up the night before.

Like the previous night, it was pitch black out. The moon hid behind the horizon. I switched on my flashlight and studied the map.

"How far?" Alik asked.

I estimated the distance. "Should be there in ten minutes or so."

"Think we should park on the side of the road and walk down the unmarked lane?"

"He said it was a quarter mile, right?"

Alik nodded.

"Take us five minutes or so. Probably a good idea. If anyone is patrolling, we might hear them."

We passed through another small town. A few streetlights cast orange orbs on the ground. A couple kids hung out nearby, smoking something. They attempted to hide it as we passed.

"You smoke grass as a kid?" I asked Alik.

"What?"

"Marijuana."

"No." He paused a beat. "You?"

I shrugged. "Maybe."

"Does it really matter?"

"Guess not. Making conversation is all."

Soon we were in the darkness again. I spotted a narrow dirt road the moment we passed it.

"I think that was it."

"Where?"

"Back there."

"Shit."

"Just pull over here."

"Should I go back?"

"No. If someone is listening out, they might think it odd for a car to drive by, stop, and turn around. Just go another couple hundred yards and pull over."

A few seconds later, we stopped. Alik cut the engine. The ticking of muffler was barely audible over the sounds of insects.

"Think they noticed the car shutting off?" Alik asked.

"Depends on where they are," I said. "If they're at the house, then I doubt they even noticed we drove by."

I had my fingers on the handle, about to exit, when a car pulled up behind us.

# 12

ALIK PULLED THE PISTOL FROM HIS WAISTBAND AND GLANCED AT his side mirror. There was no passenger side mirror, and the angles on the others were off, so I stared straight ahead and trusted in Alik for a few moments. The headlights washed over us and the surrounding brush. A car door opened and slammed shut. The vehicle behind us idled.

Someone approached, speaking in Greek. I was careful to pay attention to my side of the car in case someone approached, using the brush as cover. The man appeared in Alik's window. His hair was white. In the dim lighting, shadows deepened his wrinkles. He spoke, but I had no idea what he said. But his smile and tone put me at ease.

Alik responded slowly in Greek. The old guy straightened up, placed his hands on his hips. I leaned over and saw him look up and down the road. He bent over again.

"Are you sure?" He spoke in English, at the same pace as Alik.

"Yes," Alik said. "We're fine. Just stopped because we were in the middle of an intense debate."

The guy looked at me, then Alik, smiled and turned away.

I wondered whether the arrival of another car, the doors slamming, the old guy talking, if it all had alerted the men at the house to our presence.

"This is fucked," Alik said. He stared at the rearview mirror, obviously sharing in my concerns.

"We'll lay low for a bit," I said. "Get out of the car and wait on the other side of the road for fifteen. If they don't come by then, then no one paid attention to it."

We remained inside until the old guy pulled away. The area darkened and night settled in. The steady hum of insects rose again. After exiting Esau's car, we darted across the road, and made our way down toward the turn off. We found a line of hedges and took cover behind them.

Fifteen minutes passed. My eyes adjusted to the darkness. There was no sign of activity on the road or the lane that led to the house. No voices carried on the wind. No lights swept across the dirt.

"Let's go," Alik whispered.

He took the left side. I stayed on the right. Passed by the wooden pole and sign Esau had mentioned. We kept six to ten feet of distance between us. We were close enough to hear the other whisper, and could tell when the other stopped.

I felt exposed out there with nothing other than the old wooden sap for protection. Hell, I wasn't sure the pistol Esau had lent to Alik could be trusted to fire when the trigger was pulled. For all I knew, we both held bludgeoning weapons. They'd do no good if the men came at us with pistols and rifles.

Even baseball bats would give them a slight advantage. If they knew how to use them, at least.

The road continued past the bushes. On either side were overgrown fields that moved with the wind. The house stood in the distance. A single-story square structure. It was too dark to tell what kind of condition it was in. The windows were dark. It didn't appear to have a garage and there weren't any cars parked in front.

Alik got my attention and signaled for us to move to the rear of the house. I followed his lead. There weren't cars in back, either. They must've left Isadora here with a couple of men, then left.

Or they had left her corpse here.

Being more than a thousand feet off the road, and with no neighbors, the house was the kind of place you could torture and kill and no one would ever know.

I caught up to Alik. "Let's get closer and check the windows."

We cut across the lawn to the rear corner of the house. Made our way around counter-clockwise. The windows were darkened with drapes. Switching on our flashlights to peek through the cracks was out. It would draw attention. But luck intervened. On the far side, one of the windows had been left open. We stood there for five minutes, listening. There wasn't a sound from within.

"Cover me." I pushed the window up and parted the drapes. Best I could tell, the room was empty. "I'm going in."

Alik stepped up behind me, pistol extended, ready to shove it through the opening if someone came after me.

I went up and over and I rolled through to the floor with the sap in hand. My ribs burned. My hip, too. I buried the pain. It was warm inside, and smelled like garbage.

We waited with me inside and Alik out for another few minutes. No one approached. The door to the room didn't open. Everything remained still. My eyes adjusted and a few dark outlines of furniture appeared.

"It's clear," I said.

Alik climbed in and switched on his flashlight after covering it with the window treatment in an effort to reduce the brightness. It provided enough light to see a few feet ahead. Probably made the window glow from outside. He panned around the room. There was a bed and a dresser and a bunch of trash on the floor, but nothing else. He focused the diffused beam on the door. I pulled it open. Alik stuck his arm through. We waited, then both stepped into an open room. There was a tipped over couch near the far wall. The skeleton of a kitchen against the back wall. A bare kitchen table next to it.

And two closed doors opposite where we stood.

"Which one?" Alik whispered.

I switched on my light and aimed it left. Started toward it.

Alik grabbed my shoulder. "Are you prepared for what we might find in there?"

"Yes."

I turned the knob and pushed the door open. The room smelled like decomposing flesh. It made me gag. I had to back up and swallow air before entering. I shoved my light into the gap and pulled the cloth away from the lens. There were three black trash bags on the floor in the middle of the room. Nothing else.

Alik moved in, grabbed one, and dumped it on the floor. Loose trash spilled out. Flies buzzed. Maggots withered on the ground. He poured out the second bag, then the third. There were papers, rotten meat, left over food, paper plates. Some of the stuff could have been there for months.

But no body.

We left the room and shut the door, both of us with our forearms up to our mouths to silence the coughing and gagging.

"No way someone's here," I said. "They'd have come out already."

Alik forced himself to swallow as he headed toward the last door. He opened it a crack and held his pistol in the gap.

"Whoever's in there, we have you surrounded," he said.

No one responded.

He placed his flashlight above the pistol and kicked the door open. I waited a few feet away as he entered the room. I prepared my mind for the worst. Alik would come out, shaking his head, avoiding eye contact. He would tell me they killed her, sparing the details of how.

And like a fool, I'd rush past him to see for myself.

The door creaked open. I aimed my light at it. Alik stepped out, shaking his head, taking a deep breath. He looked up at me.

"Spit it out," I said.

"Empty," he said.

"Shit." Relief washed over me. The sweat on my skin felt cold for a second.

I stepped around him and peered into the room. Four plain walls and the bare subfloor, blackened with mold. The carpet had been ripped up and tack strips left behind. Nails poked out like a medieval torture device. Other than that, nothing. Where was she? We had cleared the house and found nothing. I turned and walked past Alik and stood in the middle of the room. Alik was looking up.

"Attic?" I said.

"Didn't see an access," he said.

"I didn't check the room we came in through."

We headed back the way we came in. I was swinging my flashlight across the floor, up the walls, over the ceiling. Maybe we had missed a lot stalking through the house.

Alik entered the room ahead of me. His light lit it up. He spun to meet me.

"Nothing," he said.

"Figures," I said. Then I thought of something else. "Come with me."

I went back to the middle of the main room and stopped and waited for him.

"What is it?" he asked.

I lifted my knee and held it in the air a moment. My hip tightened with pain. My right leg hurt like hell. Figured I had re-injured one of the fractures. But it didn't affect my balance, so I stood still for a second, then I drove my foot to the ground like I was trying to break through the planks of wood we stood on.

The sound was hollow and soft. If we were on a slab, it would have been solid. The floor reverberated under the force of my kick.

"Hear that?" I said. "Feel it?"

Alik nodded, slowly, as though he got it too.

"There's a space below us," I said.

"Where's the cellar access?" he said.

I retraced our steps around the house. We hadn't split up. Our lack of firepower prevented it. I hadn't seen a door outside leading underground, and neither had Alik. The only two doors were in front and back and from where I stood in the middle of the room I had a sight line to both.

"Could it be out in the field?" Alik said.

"Why?"

"I don't know." He leaned his head back and stared at the ceiling like the answer was spray painted there. "Can't think of any reason someone would want a tunnel into a basement."

"Only one going out," I said. "But if that were the only method of ingress and egress, it would defeat the purpose."

"Which is?"

"A way to get away. Think about it. These men, they aren't exactly lined up on the right side of the law, right? So it makes sense they would want some kind of way to escape sight unseen. A tunnel leading out of the basement makes sense, then. Right?"

"But how do they get down there?"

"Exactly."

"OK, scratch that idea, then." Alik walked into the kitchen area. He moved chairs, pushed the table to the wall, stomped on the floor. "What are we missing?"

"Dunno. Place ain't that big."

I walked up next to him and stared at the cooking area. There was a two burner stove. Counter space. A single sink. Grime coated the fixtures. A couple cabinets had been nailed in haste to the walls. Someone had painted them black at some point. The paint was streaked and faded.

Alik opened the cabinets. They were empty.

"The fridge," I said.

He moved in front of it.

"It's crooked," I said.

He grabbed hold and pulled it back. "Son of a bitch."

## 13

"There's our access."

The door was five feet high, and two and a half feet wide. It had a deadbolt, a chain lock, and swung inward. Alik checked the handle and the door didn't budge.

"Help me move this fridge out of the way," Alik said.

We dragged it across the floor and left it next to the table. Alik rushed forward and delivered a front kick that landed next to the knob. The door and frame splintered and cracked and separated. The hunk of wood swung hard into the wall. The hinges creaked as it floated back toward us.

Alik descended the weathered stairs first. I was on his tail. The air smelled musty. My fingers traced the wall, slick with condensation. Alik's light aimed down. Mine to the side. By the time I cleared the ceiling, Alik was on the ground. I took the remaining steps two at a time.

"Where the hell is she?" Alik said.

The narrow space between the stairs and exterior wall

wasn't big enough for the both us, and Alik wasn't moving. So I pushed him forward and then past him as we stepped into the cellar. The floor was concrete in some spots. Dirt in others. The air was stagnant. Water trickled down the walls in a couple spots, turning the floor into mud where it fell.

In the middle of the room was a tipped over chair. Rope was tied to the back. It had been sawed through. But that wasn't the worst of it. A few feet away, underneath where the back door stood above us, I saw a shirt. A white blouse with red thread woven down the buttons. Buttons that weren't attached to the shirt anymore. Buttons I saw scattered around the room as I panned my light on the floor. The thread wasn't the only thing red on the blouse, either. There were blood streaks and spatters. I picked it up and held it to my face and inhaled.

"Lavender."

"What?" Alik was walking toward me.

"Isadora wore lavender perfume. Or, rather, it was in her shampoo, but her hair hung over her shoulders. Left the fragrance behind on her shirt."

He nodded and turned and shone his light in the space under the stairs. He took a few steps, bent over and picked something up.

"What's that?" I asked.

He turned and held out a dirty, yellow, folded piece of paper. I took it and held my light over it.

"A pamphlet?"

"Looks that way."

"It's written in Greek." I handed it back to Alik. "What's it say?"

"I can barely speak the language. You think I can read it?"

"Better than I can."

He studied the paper for a few moments, unfolding and refolding it. He tapped on the front of it. "Something medical. Some kind of clinic, I think."

I took the pamphlet back and unfolded it, studied it, refolded it. There was something scrawled in pencil on the back.

"Any idea what that says?" I asked him.

Alik shook his head. "I can't make out most of the print. You think I can figure out the handwriting?"

We were getting nowhere, so I folded the pamphlet in thirds and stuck it in my back pocket. Looking around the room, I wondered if we'd seen Isadora for the last time. The blood on her shirt had dried. They'd torn it off her a while ago. We were a couple hours behind, at least. And we had no idea where they might've taken her.

Alik led the way up the stairs. We rigged the door so it wouldn't fall open and repositioned the fridge in front of it. We walked through the house one last time in search of anything that might indicate where they had gone next. But in the end we found nothing.

Exiting through the back door, I was hit with humid air and the soft hum of insects. Thought I might've heard waves crashing. But it only happened twice. And it came from north. Which was the wrong direction considering we were on the southern side of the island.

"Cars," I said.

"I know," Alik said.

We stayed in the field until we reached the brush. It was too thick to walk through, so we took the dirt road and stayed close to the side until we reached the main road. It was pitch black. We took turns looking back in hopes that we could spot a car coming before they saw us. The thickets might hurt going in, but it was better than being caught by the guys who had taken Isadora.

I couldn't help but think allowing that to happen might be the best option, considering we had no idea where they had gone.

*Take me to her. Please. I'll make you pay.*

The car remained where we had left it. My window was cranked down an inch. Alik's up all the way. We got in and eased our doors closed. They weren't latched, but we'd do that while moving to reduce the effects of the sound in the still night.

Alik turned the key in the ignition. The little engine revved high then settled in. He eased off the clutch and pressed the gas and we pulled away. But the movement was jerky, and it sounded like a herd of horses galloped behind us.

"Shit," he said, stopping on the side of the road.

I opened my door and had a foot on the ground before we'd halted. I directed my light toward the rear of the car. Got out, checked the front. Walked around the bumper and checked the driver's side. The front was OK.

But the back driver's side tire not so much.

Alik had rolled down his window and hung his head out the opening.

"Flat?"

"Yeah." I walked past him and knelt by the tire and worked my hand around it. "I could be wrong, but feels like someone slashed it."

Alik got out. He slammed his door shut and then kicked it. "Think it was them?"

"Maybe."

"They drove by, saw a car out there, maybe knew it was Esau's?"

"I think if they knew it was Esau's, we'd have been paid a visit."

"Kids, then?"

"Maybe."

"We heard a couple cars passing when we left the house, right?"

"I preferred to think of them as waves, but, yeah, we heard them."

"Think they could have done it?"

"Maybe."

"Can't you think of anything else to say, Jack?"

"What's to say, man? Someone slashed the tire. We didn't see them. As far as I can tell, they're gone. If it had been someone with mal intent, they'd have slapped us while we were standing here bitching at each other."

"Shit." Alik kicked the side of the car again, then reached inside and pulled out the keys. He popped the trunk and pulled out a small donut wheel and a tool bag.

By the time we finished changing the tire, sweat was dripping down my face. My mouth felt parched. Didn't matter the air had a cool bite to it. The humidity overpowered it.

"What now?" Alik said.

"Guess we return the car." I rolled down my window and leaned into the wind rush as Alik whipped the car around and accelerated. "And give Esau the bad news."

## 14

Esau hadn't taken the news well. He had opened the door and saw the two of us standing there. He rose on his tiptoes and craned his head side to side. Then he settled back and his eyes went wet and his shoulders slumped. He looked down at the floor.

"Sorry, Esau," I had said.

He was shaking his head when he'd closed the door on us.

We took the car back into town and left it on the street near the cafe. Then we slept.

I woke up after sunrise, wearing the same clothes from the night before. My body was stiff and full of aches. My ribs were visibly bruised. So was my hip. Black and blue and painful to the touch. I stretched it out and after a few minutes lumbered from my room to the living room. The window was open, but the air was still. Alik stood at the counter, drinking coffee and turning eggs over in a pan.

"Felt like cooking this morning?" I asked.

"Cafe's closed still," he said.

"Mind making a few of those for me?"

He lifted the pan and tipped three eggs with their yolks intact onto a plate. Steam caught a band of sunlight and rose in swirling wisps.

"These are for you."

I poured a cup of coffee and grabbed the plate off the counter while the ceramic mug burned my fingertips. I set both on the table and eased into a chair. A few sips of the brew and the fog lifted. A couple bites of food and the ache in my stomach faded. The rest of my pains remained.

Alik sat down and buried his face in his hands for a moment. Then he looked up at me and asked how the food was. I nodded and grunted as I took a bite. Alik nodded in response.

"I'm worried about Esau," he said.

"Me too," I said, perhaps with too much egg in my mouth. I felt a piece hit my chin on the way to the table.

He was shaking his head as he looked away for a moment. "What if they were out there, Jack?"

"Where? The house?"

"The road. Just far enough away we wouldn't see them, but they could watch the car. Watch us. See us changing the tire. Then follow us back to his house."

"Crossed my mind, too."

"And now Esau's not here. He's always here early."

"Situations dictate behavior." I washed my mouth with coffee, set the mug down. "I'd say things are different now. His focus is on Isadora, not his business."

"Think we should check on him?"

Scooping the final scraps of eggs into my mouth, I nodded. "I need to change first."

Alik rose, grabbed the keys. "Hurry."

I splashed some water on my face, then changed into a pair of tan cargo shorts and a blue and white checkered shirt. Alik was waiting in the hall when I exited the bathroom. I slipped on a pair of sandals. We hurried downstairs, checking the cafe to see if Esau had made it in. The lights and equipment were off. The office empty.

We ducked out the side entrance. I glanced over. There were a few old guys waiting outside the cafe door. They smoked, joked, leaned back against the glass and appeared relaxed. Sometimes schedules were discarded in the small town. They knew that. They were OK with that. It's one of the reasons they had remained when their siblings and friends had left for opportunities elsewhere.

The car sat where we had left it, one corner lower to the ground due to the spare tire. But at least all the tires looked full of air. Alik hopped in and started it up. Esau's house wasn't situated far from town, so the drive only took a couple minutes. The warm air rushed in the car and washed over me. Was as close as I was getting to a shower for a while.

Gravel crunched underneath the wheels as we turned onto the driveway. The old man opened the door before we were out of the car.

"Was wondering when you would show up," he said, slamming his front door behind him. He spun and inserted a key then limped across the yard.

I got out and slid my seat forward so he could get in back.

"Everything OK?" I said.

"Huh?" he said.

I looked down at his leg. "You're limping."

"Ah, yes, it flares up, time to time. Old injury from the war."

"One day you're gonna have to tell me all about that war."

He nodded and said nothing.

I said, "After we get Isadora back, of course."

Esau stopped and stared at me with a weak smile plastered on his face. Then he got in the car.

"I've made some arrangements," Esau said.

"What kind?" I said.

"Weapons for the two of you. Things are just crazy here. And while I'd prefer to get you off the island, I need your help too much. Obviously, I can't do this alone."

"When will they be here?"

"Later today. Worst case, tomorrow."

"Tomorrow might be too late." I looked back at him. "Hell, right now might be too late."

Esau looked away. His lips drew tight. None of us wanted to think about it, but it was there. Alik and I had seen it, and we'd told Esau about it, and that was all there was to it. Every minute that passed meant we were closer to finding out Isadora didn't make it.

Alik pulled in front of the cafe. The crowd looked at the car, then us. They pushed off the glass when they saw Esau. They patted their bellies and slapped each other on the back.

Esau beat them back like wild animals as he unlocked the front door. The old men shuffled in and seated themselves at tables.

Things changed fast. The day before, no one would come in. Now they couldn't wait. Hadn't they heard about Isadora? Hadn't they seen? Maybe that was the reason they were there. These people weren't just customers, they were Esau's friends. They'd shown up to support the old man.

Esau stepped out of the office and went behind the counter

and started the grill. He pulled pastries out of the fridge and set them on plates. He started a few pots of coffee. After a few minutes, he had several plates on the counter, each with an accompanying mug. Then Esau slipped into the office again.

The old men walked up to the counter, took a plate, dropped some money next to the register, and returned to their tables. Forks banged against plates. Mugs were lifted and set down with soft thuds. Chairs scraped the floor.

The bells hanging from the front door jingled. I shot a glance toward it. A boy maybe ten or eleven years old entered. He stood just inside the entrance, hopping on one foot to the other like he needed an invitation to use the bathroom or he was going to piss all over the floor.

Esau came back out of the office. After some quick banter with one of the men, he spotted the boy and froze in place.

The boy's eyes widened and he nodded and pulled a folded envelope from his pocket. He hurried over to Esau and handed it to him. Esau stared down at the plain white envelope for a moment as the boy turned and darted toward the door. Esau reached out, but missed. The boy raced past me. I didn't make an attempt to stop him.

Esau shuffled over to the table with the envelope in hand. He held it a foot or so away from his body. His face was tight. Eyes unblinking. He fell back into the chair opposite mine.

I looked at the door as it swung shut. The kid had hurried out of sight. Where were the men who had sent him? I rose, ready to go check.

"Wait," Esau said. His voice was weak and thready. He cleared his throat. "Wait a moment. Please."

By this time, Alik had joined us. We waited for the old man to open the envelope or hand it to one of us to do so. After a few seconds, he peeled back the flap and retrieved a yellow piece of paper torn from a spiral notebook. Little tags of frayed paper lined the top. The letter written in pencil.

Esau mumbled as he read it. Then he covered his eyes and shook his head.

"What's it say?" I said.

Esau said nothing.

I nodded at Alik. He pried the paper from Esau and stared at it.

"Well?" I said.

"Not sure what it says other than the numbers," Alik said.

Esau said, "I don't have that kind of money."

My first thought was, Isadora's alive. My second thought was how much money?

"They are asking for the equivalent of five hundred thousand U.S. dollars."

"They wouldn't ask that if they didn't think you had it," I said. "So why do they think you have it?"

He said nothing.

"Esau, what did you do?"

"And that's not all," Esau said, ignoring the question. "It says they want the good Samaritan to deliver it. Alone."

I glanced at Alik.

He said, "That's you, Jack."

"Figured as much." I gestured at the paper, which had been set on the table. "Where?"

"It doesn't say," Esau said. "Only mentions they'll let us know around seven."

I glanced at my watch. It was eight thirty in the morning. "So tonight, then. Can you see if your contact can get here sooner?"

Esau nodded.

"One more thing," I said.

"What?" Esau said.

"If you want me to go through with this, I need more details."

Esau glanced around, nodded, rose. "Come to my office. Both of you."

## 15

It was the first time I'd been in the cafe's office. It smelled like stale coffee and donuts. Four small panel windows allowed light in. Wasn't much to the room. An old wooden desk, cluttered with several stacks of paper, some as tall as eight inches high. An old computer monitor on one end, set at an angle. A dying plant next to it. A large desk calendar turned to the wrong month. That didn't matter much. The calendar itself was three years old. There were scribbles all over it. Names and places, I figured. Phone numbers from around the globe.

Esau walked around the desk and took a seat in a beat-up office chair. Alik and I sat opposite him in metal fold-up chairs that had little padding left on the seat. The metal rail dug into my back. I shifted until I managed some level of comfort.

"I was sixteen in 1949," Esau said. "My best friend, Kostas, was nineteen. He was like an older brother to me. He'd enlisted in the Hellenic Army to fight in the war against the DSE forces." He paused, glanced at each of us, and added, "It was the Civil

War. The communists, including the Soviets, backed the DSE and the Greek Communist Party."

"I've seen documentaries," I said. "Not the most pleasant of times for your country."

Esau shook his head. "No, it was not. Christ, is it for any country? Anyway, Kostas joined up and made it in time for the Battle of Leonidio. And, well, he wrote back to me about it and I was entranced. I wanted to be a part of it. So I lied and told them I was my brother who would have been nineteen at the time if he hadn't drowned the summer I was ten. Back in those days they needed men and didn't question things like that. The next day, they shipped me off for some training. Within a month, I was reunited with Kostas, and was present for two of the three final battles."

"OK. What's this have to do with—"

"I'm getting to that." Esau sipped from his mug, set it down, and folded his hands in his lap. He leaned back in his chair and closed his eyes. The wrinkles on his face sagged. "I can still picture the things we did. Countrymen killing countrymen. Worse than that, at times. Unspeakable things. Did your documentary cover that?"

He opened his eyes. They were covered with a thin film of mist.

I'd seen enough during my time at war that I didn't need him to recount the details. I nodded. Saw Alik do the same.

Esau returned the gesture. "We never left each other's side during those battles. We had made a pact, if one of us dies, the other would avenge him. And if we both died, well at least we'd go together." He smiled for a second. "In those days, there were no loves of our lives. It was girl of the week, if you know what I mean. We were everything to each other. And we fought like it.

I can't count how many times he saved my ass. And I know I kept a bullet or knife or bayonet from slicing through his skin more than a couple times."

He paused for a few moments. Forks clattering against plates and mugs pounding the tables in the dining room filled the silent void.

"So after the war, I was still a kid and he had turned twenty. I decided to come home. He stayed in the military for a while longer. Got stationed elsewhere, and over time we lost touch."

"Happens all the time," I said, remembering far too many friends I hadn't spoken to in years. How many thought I was dead now? How many cared?

"I suppose," Esau said. "And when we did catch up, it was always apparent how far apart the paths we had taken were."

"Such as?"

"Me? I became a businessman. Opened a few restaurants in various places and then came here to retire. A farce, really. Because you can't just stop doing what you love, right?" He paused, waiting for our acknowledgment. "So I opened this place with our savings."

"And what of your friend?" Alik asked.

"He became a businessman of a different sort," Esau said.

"A criminal," I said.

Esau nodded. "Drugs, racketeering, smuggling. His own import, export, security services company, I guess. Started small, as most do, I suppose. Grew it quite large. He's a powerful man now."

"How close have you two been since 1950?" Alik asked.

"We haven't talked regularly," Esau said. "But, when you have two people who went through the things we did together, well, that takes the edge off of the decades. You know?"

I watched him fidget with a pen for a few moments. "Did you ever work for him?"

Esau seemed taken aback by the question. "I've never been a criminal in my life. God knows I could have used the easy money. And it's not like he never offered. But I couldn't see myself doing that."

"You lied to get into the army," I said.

His cheeks burned red and he narrowed his eyes at me. "I did that to help defend my family and the families of those around me. Damned if the communists were going to take over my country and dictate my future."

I raised a hand. "Fair enough. I'm just trying to get a handle on where this is going. Only thing I can figure after you telling this story is that you burned the guy at some point in the past, and now he's collecting. Either the money or your niece's head. I want to know why."

Esau eased back in his chair again. His face went slack. The color drained from his cheeks. His eyelids dropped shut. He was completely still. If it weren't for his ragged breathing, the result of his crooked nose, I would have thought he had died on the spot.

"The doctors said my wife, Eleni, would fare better by the sea. And an island setting like this would be best. No pollution. Less shit in the air. They felt this combined with regular treatments would be the way to cure her lung cancer. And it worked, for a while. It helped extend her life years past her original check out date."

I'd heard the other side of the story from Isadora. Eleni's sickness was the reason Isadora had come here years ago. After the woman passed, Isadora had hung around to help. Out of guilt, I supposed.

Esau continued. "When things got real bad, I mean, coughing blood, unstoppable coughing fits, pain beyond belief, they told me the only option was a radical procedure. The cancer had spread, you see, and they said the only way to stop it was this operation. Well, it cost over one hundred thousand U.S. dollars."

"And you didn't have that kind of money lying around," I said.

He shook his head. "I'd tied what we had into the house and into this cafe. As much as we like to think our assets are liquid, the economy made it impossible to sell them quickly enough. And even if I had managed to, what then? She'd be healed, maybe, and we would be out of a home and business."

"So you turned to the one guy you knew had the kind of money you needed."

"Not at first. I begged family. Tried to take out a second loan on the business and the house. Sold off some things, collectibles, old items I'd treasured. In the end, I came up with ten thousand dollars. So, like you said, I took a plane, and a train, and rented a car, and visited my old friend. It was the first time I had seen him in over thirteen years. He'd aged better than I had. He had all the stress in the world, but you couldn't tell it by looking at him."

"What did he say when you asked?" Alik said.

"He told me no problem. Sent one of his guys to the safe. The guy returned with a suitcase with the money. That was it."

"What kind of terms did he offer you?" I said.

Esau glanced up at the ceiling, smiled, shook his head, said, "Pay it back when you can."

"And this was a few years back, right?" I said.

He nodded, said nothing.

"And how much have you paid him?" Alik said.

Esau looked away. Cleared his throat. Muttered something.

"Didn't catch that," I said.

Esau stared me down. "I said nothing."

"And these men who've been bothering you?"

"His guys."

"I thought so." I looked at Alik for a moment, then back at Esau. "What was the arrangement again?"

Esau was fidgeting with his fingers and hesitated a moment before answering. In a meek voice, he said, "Ten thousand the first year, then twenty each year after."

"So not quite the 'pay it back when you can,' that you mentioned."

"He changed the terms on me."

"When?"

"After Eleni died."

# 16

---

ALIK AND I RETREATED TO OUR APARTMENT. WE ONLY HAD FOUR or so hours until seven. Until the instructions arrived. We spent an hour scouring the place for anything I could use as a weapon. It had to be something easy to conceal. I was about to walk into a hornet's nest, dealing with men who worked for one of Greece's biggest criminals. Damned if I was doing it naked.

We went over the things Esau had said. It added up, to a point. He spoke of their friendship in a way that nothing could break the bond. I knew what it was like to bleed with a friend. To risk everything to save their life, and have them do the same in return. My old partner Bear could call me any time of day or night, and from anywhere in the world, and I'd show up in a heartbeat even if it meant taking a bullet for him.

And while a hundred thousand was a lot of money, it sounded like peanuts to Kostas. I could see him shaking down his old friend to instill a bit of fear as payback, but then writing it off as a bad debt and moving on. Why go after Esau like this? Hell, why go after Isadora? If Esau had the money, he'd have paid. There was nothing to gain here.

"Maybe he's got the cash somewhere," I said.

Alik stopped what he was doing and turned to me. "Why do you say that?"

"Why else would this guy kidnap Isadora? If Esau can't pay up, they gotta kill her. What good does that do anyone? Just take *him* out and be done with it."

"They want him to suffer," Alik said.

"He's already lost his wife," I said.

"Guess it's possible he didn't care about her."

"He moved here for her."

"I don't know, Jack. I don't care. I hate how far this has gone. I think we need to scrap this plan and call the police."

"No. We do that, Isadora dies."

"We don't do that and you die. Then her. Then Esau. And maybe me after that. If they don't get me, Frank Skinner will."

"So leave if that's what you're afraid of."

"I'm not afraid, Jack. I just don't want to see you killed over something that isn't your battle."

"I've made it my battle."

"Why?" He held his hands up and had a dumbfounded look on his face.

"Haven't you ever found yourself so close to a situation that you took on the problem as your own?"

"Sure, but with people I knew and cared for."

"So maybe I care for Esau."

"You and I both know that's bullshit, Jack."

I shrugged. "Maybe you're right. I do care for Isadora, though."

"Why? You hardly know her."

"I know her well enough. She reminds me of someone back home. A woman I was entrusted to take care of. A woman I've been in and out of love with for years."

"And are you in or out right now?"

"Not sure. Haven't had time to think about it."

Alik laughed. "You've had all the time in the world while stuck up here nursing your wounds."

I shrugged, said nothing.

"We should call the cops," he said.

"We can't."

"So we do nothing?"

"No, I go wherever Kostas wants me to go."

"Esau hasn't even agreed. And it sounds like he doesn't have the money, so what's the point?"

"He doesn't need it."

"You think you can take on all these men by yourself?"

"Probably not."

Alik took a seat on the couch. "Then we have to come up with a way for me to follow you."

"That could get us all killed."

"We're all dead anyway. Might as well be proactive about it."

I crossed the room and stood in front of the window and lifted it open. Warm air billowed past, carrying the scent of a fresh catch. Down the coast four fishing vessels were pulling in.

"We should go see Esau," I said.

We left the apartment, headed down the stairs, stepped into the cafe. It was a quarter full, with half the patrons on the terrace. The old men looked away as we made the short trip to Esau's office.

He was sitting in his ratty chair, head leaned back, his eyes fixed on the ceiling.

I rapped my knuckles against his door.

Esau didn't move.

I knocked again. Alik cleared his throat.

"What?" Esau said, his voice raspy.

"Have you thought about what you are going to do?" Alik asked.

"Do?" Esau's head rolled forward. His hands lifted from his lap and he draped them and his arms over his desk. He looked up from his hunched posture. "What do you mean, what am I going to do? You talk as though I have options here."

"You have some," I said.

"What?"

"They want me. You can send me."

"Empty handed? You'll be a dead man."

"If they can kill me."

"No offense, Jack," Esau said. "I understand who you are and the things you have done. But you are a shell of that man right now."

Alik placed his hand on my shoulder. I shrugged it off.

I said, "I'm the best option you've got unless you're willing to trade your life for hers. Are you prepared to do that?"

Esau looked down at the space between his steepled hands. His tongue clicked as he licked his lips. A grunt of a word slipped out.

"No."

"That's what I thought."

He looked up, eyebrows raised, forehead folded into a dozen wrinkles. "So what do we do?"

"How much cash do you have lying around?"

Esau glanced up at the ceiling. His gaze remained fixed. He wasn't mentally counting or thinking about his bank accounts.

"What's up there?" Alik said.

Esau shrugged, said nothing.

I grabbed one of the fold-up chairs and placed it in the middle of the room. The chair looked like it could hold a guy maybe half my size. I ignored the pain in my hip and planted my left leg on it. Pressed down. Wiggled side to side to inch the chair closer to center.

"Be ready to catch me," I said to Alik. Then I stepped up and angled my head to the right to keep from hitting the ceiling with it. I extended both arms and pushed the ceiling tile up and set it to the right. I stuck my head into the hole. It was dark and dusty and smelled like coffee and donuts, just like Esau's office.

"See anything?" Esau asked.

I blinked and my eyes adjusted to the light. In front of me there was nothing. To the right, nothing. Same on the opposite side. I shuffled in a circle on the chair like a ballerina until I was a hundred and eighty degrees from where I started.

"There it is," I said.

"What?" Alik said.

"Found it," I said, pulling my head out of the hole. I jumped off the chair. Slid it five feet toward the door, then hopped back up. This tile took a little more force to move. I punched the corners a couple times to free it. Then I reached into the attic and grabbed the canvas bag. It was heavy and full so that the sides puffed out. It slid across the tile with a hiss. I leaned to the side and lowered it down to Alik, then rejoined him on the ground.

"How much is in there?" Alik asked Esau.

The old man shrugged and looked away.

"Count it," I said to Alik.

Dust rose as he slapped the bag. He wiped off the zipper and pulled it back. Reached inside and grabbed a brick of bills.

"It's about twenty thousand U.S.," Esau said.

"Not near enough," Alik said.

"But it might buy us Isadora's life," I said.

"Or it might get yours extinguished," Alik said.

"Maybe, but that's a chance I'm willing to take."

Alik set the bag on the chair and shoved his hands in his pockets. He looked past me at Esau. "It should be you going, old man. You should own up to your mistake."

Esau rose, cheeks burning. He aimed a loaded finger at Alik. "I did what he asked. How was I supposed to know he'd call the loan like this? I don't have that kind of money just laying around."

Alik grabbed the bag and held it in front of his chest. "You had this, you old fool. You could have bought time with it. Instead you kept it squirreled away. What were you going to do with this money? Huh? Is it more important than your niece's life?"

Esau stepped around his desk and bulldozed his way toward Alik. He grabbed hold of the bag and started yanking. Wads of cash fell to the floor. The old man yelled and swung and stumbled and crashed into the wall and fell to the floor.

Footsteps echoed into the office like rumbling thunder. Five old men stood outside the door, staring in.

"It's all right, fellas," I said.

Esau sat up. Wiped the sweat from his brow. He looked at the guys and waved them off. "It's OK."

The men retreated. I closed the door and stood between Esau and Alik. I held the men at arm's length.

"This is how this is gonna go. I'm taking this money. And Esau, if you have any more, you better let me know. I don't care if it's cash, stocks, bonds, a title to a house in Siberia, I want it available to negotiate with."

He shook his head. "That's all I got other than the house and this place, and there's no equity in either."

I glanced at Alik. He shrugged. We had to take the old man at his word, which wasn't that solid.

"Fair enough, I guess. We're gonna get the call or message or carrier pigeon or whatever at seven. That's four hours from now. I need to rest up. Esau, you do whatever you can to get me a decent weapon. One for Alik, too."

"They said alone," Esau said.

"I know," I said.

"Let us handle that part of it," Alik said.

## 17

SOMEHOW I MANAGED TO SLEEP FOR THREE HOURS. I WOKE UP A quarter after six as the sun dipped low behind the building, casting shadows over the terrace and the rocky beach. The wind had picked up. So had the waves. The sound of them crashing against the shore carried up the side of the building and rumbled in the apartment.

I started a pot of coffee and pulled some cooked ground lamb out of the fridge. Poured some olive oil in a cast iron skillet. Heated it all up. By the time the coffee was ready, so was the meat.

The muted light and sound of the rolling waves made it feel as though I was at a yoga retreat. It helped clear my cluttered mind. I isolated my thoughts and destroyed them one at a time until all I had left was the sequence of events ahead of me. Problem was, after arriving at the location they were to provide at seven, I had no idea how things would go. There were too many unknown variables.

Sure, I could visualize the ideal scenario, at least for the situation. But what then? What if there was a wild card? That, I told myself, was my specialty. I was the guy who they sent in when the mission had no set path to reach the objective. Getting Isadora back was no different. It required the specific mix of talent that I brought to the table.

The door opened up as I dropped my fork on the empty plate. Swirls of olive oil remained. Alik walked in. He carried a plain brown bag in one arm. The canvas money bag in the other.

"He cleaned out his bank account," Alik said. "Another three grand for you to use."

I nodded. "Weapons?"

"Got a Beretta M9 for you." He reached into the brown bag and pulled out the pistol and set it next to my plate, muzzle facing the wall.

I picked up the weapon and inspected it. Ejected the magazine. Racked the slide. It felt cool against my hand. Smelled freshly oiled.

"Good?" Alik said.

"It'll do," I said. "He come up with something for you?"

"Same weapon."

"Good enough, I suppose." I stood, tucked the pistol in my waistband, grabbed my mug and my plate and carried them over to the sink and set them there. "Anything else?"

"A cell phone."

"You keep it. Write down the number so I can memorize it."

Keys jingled. "Have to use his car."

"He get the spare replaced?"

"No."

"Hope I don't have to drive too far."

"Do what you got to do, Jack."

I turned and met his gaze. "I am."

Alik walked to the window. The wind lifted his hair and tugged at his clothing. "I suppose we should head downstairs now."

"Guess so."

He led the way through the apartment, down the hallway and stairs, into the cafe. There were a dozen or so patrons there. The old guys had retreated. Families now sat around the tables. Moms and dads and kids. Were they oblivious to what had happened in there?

Esau stood behind the counter. His drawn face didn't move as I approached. No smile, no hello, no wink or lift of the eyebrow or dip of the chin. His eyes looked sunken, surrounded by black circles.

I approached and stopped in front of him. He still didn't acknowledge me. "Anything yet?"

Esau spent a long moment staring over my shoulder, ignoring my presence. Then he blinked and his gaze swept slowly and met mine.

"No," he said.

I took a seat next to Alik in the midway through the room against the back wall. We both leaned against it, giving us a view of the front and back of the cafe. No one could come in from the terrace unless they fought the breakers and the rocks and scaled the ten-foot high wall. But perhaps they had already planted the courier and he waited outside.

At five to seven, a family of five rose from their table and headed toward the door. The dad looked back at us, focused on me. He furrowed his brow and narrowed his eyes. Had I seen him before? I scanned the recesses of my mind trying to find a match for the guy. There were plenty that looked like him. Average height. Dark hair. A little spare tire around the waist. Permanent shadow on his face. Maybe he had heard what had happened. Presumably, he blamed the stranger for it.

A few feet from the door he turned to his wife and led her through the opening. Then the family was gone and we were down to seven other diners in the cafe.

"What was that?" Alik asked.

"Hell if I know," I said.

We sat in silence for a few minutes. I looked at my watch. Two minutes to go. Glanced at the clock on the wall. A minute and a half left. My watch again. The second hand swept past twelve. I counted the seconds as they passed. I looked at Alik. He was doing the same thing.

With fifteen seconds left, the glass to the right of the front door imploded. The few people left in the cafe jumped and screamed and fell back in their chairs. A brick bounced off a table and hit the floor with a thud, chipping the tile. The brick slid a few more feet and came to a stop. Alik and I were both out of our seats, rushing toward it. He reached first. Picked it up. Held it in front of me. Two lengths of cord were wrapped around it. On the bottom, or the top, I guess, was a folded piece of paper.

Alik used a steak knife to cut the rope, then removed and unfolded the paper.

"What's it say?" I asked.

Alik motioned for Esau, who had already stepped out from behind the counter. He took the paper. It trembled in his hands.

"Step outside. Turn right. Walk one hundred meters. Get in the red car. Keys are in the glove box."

"Shit," Alik said.

"What?" Esau said.

"No destination," I said.

"What's it matter?" Esau said.

"I don't know where he's going," Alik said.

"What's it matter?" Esau said again.

"I can't be seen following him," Alik said.

"You're not going to follow," Esau said. "You're not doing a damn thing. They said alone. He has to go alone."

"Why don't you trade places with him then? Huh? You damned old fool, this is your fault anyway."

I put an arm between the men. "Alik."

"Whatever, Jack. Why are you doing this? We should call the authorities. Do this the right way. Why risk your life for this old man?" His eyes burned at Esau. "Those were nice stories about your involvement in the war, but it sounds more like you made those up or recounted someone else's experience. Nothing to live for and you still can't drag your ass out of here."

"I'm not doing it for him," I said. "I'm doing it because he's too much of a coward to risk his own life to save his niece." I turned to Esau and held up the canvas bag. "I can only get so far with this. You understand? So you'd better be ready, because I don't plan on dying."

## 18

THE WIND CLIMBED THE CAFE WALLS AND SWIRLED AROUND THE sides, whipping through the alleys. Stepping outside, it felt hot and still and humid on the sidewalk in the wash of the sunset. I heard the sound of falling raindrops and glanced back. Esau was sweeping the glass on the floor. I looked right and saw the red car parked next to a streetlight. People exited the cafe speaking in hushed tones and stepping wide of me. They headed the other direction. Seven sets of footsteps pounded the sidewalk.

I studied the windows of buildings as I made my approach. Someone had to be watching. But from where? Impossible to tell, and unless they did something stupid, like move, I might never know.

I kept my pace steady, even when passing an alley. No time to stop and enjoy the cool breeze. I was halfway to the car when headlights appeared from the end of town. They were still for a moment. The engine revved and the vehicle approached. I continued forward. The driver slowed as he passed, staring at me from behind the window. I didn't recognize the face. But that meant nothing. I had no idea how many people I was dealing with here.

The red car's muffler ticked. The scent of burned oil hung in the air. There was no condensation drip on the road. Whoever had driven it over had left the air conditioning off. Or the car didn't come equipped with it. I walked around front. Ducked down to check underneath. Kicked the tires. After opening the driver's side door, I popped the hood and the trunk and checked both. I was far from a mechanic, but it would have been obvious if someone had wired a bomb in the engine block.

At least, I hoped it would be obvious.

Everything looked normal, so I got in and shut the door. First thing I noticed was no AC. I leaned over, rolled down the passenger window, then opened the glove box and grabbed the keys. With one hand I inserted them into the ignition while rolling down my window with the other. The small engine choked and sputtered then caught and whined. I pressed the gas a couple times. The little car shook, but didn't move with the emergency brake in place.

A phone rang. Sounded like an old Greek song. I looked over and back and found the cell on the rear seat.

"Hello?"

"Underneath your seat is a GPS device. It is already powered. The destination is set. Follow it."

"OK."

"And know that we will be following you. If anyone else does the same, you will both die. So if you are in contact with your friend, be sure to tell him."

"OK."

"Don't even think about using this phone. We are monitoring it. If you so much as make a call to your mother we'll cut your hand off."

"No worries. My mother's dead."

The guy on the other end terminated the call. I tucked the phone under my left leg and reached underneath the seat. Found the GPS. It was a handheld unit. I pressed the top of the rocker button and the screen came to life. It was in navigation mode. A purple line led out of town. The device slid into a mount already fixed on the dash.

I disengaged the emergency brake and shifted into first. Pain fired through my left leg as I eased off the clutch. The car rolled forward. It lurched when I shifted into second, then smoothed out in third. The edge of town slipped past. Then Esau's neighborhood. The sun dipped behind the trees by the time I reached the small town we had passed through the night before. The kids weren't out yet. Smoke stacks rose from a couple buildings. The scent of seared meat filled the car.

Continuing along the road, I reached another familiar spot. Part of me hoped and thought this would be the destination. The abandoned house where they had taken Isadora. I knew it existed. They thought I didn't. Unless they had found out we had been there. Maybe they were watching. Maybe it was them that slashed the tire last night.

But the purple line led on, so I drove on past the dirt road, past the thicket we had parked next to, into unchartered territory. For me, at least.

The sun slipped past the horizon. Only a faint trace of orange remained near the bottom of the sky. Above and ahead it was a deepening shade of dark blue.

At the next intersection, the GPS had me turn left. Two

miles later, right. Four miles after that, left. I had no idea there were so many roads here. This side of the island had few towns. None you'd call a city. How many ways did people need to get from point A to B?

A few turns later and I was heading back the way I had come, albeit closer to the north side of the island. Perhaps there was no direct way there from town. That, or they wanted to screw with me. They wanted to watch and see what Alik would do.

The sky glowed softly orange ahead. I headed toward the artificial light. Another town? I reached the GPS and panned out a bit. It didn't show anything in that direction.

I reached the corner of a metal fence topped with barbed wire. It stretched into the darkness. The fence was on higher ground and I couldn't see what was behind it. A half mile later, lights on the ground stretched along the other side of the fence. Then a few buildings appeared. The road rose higher than the embankment and there were small planes scattered along a runway. A Gulfstream sat at the end. Lights blinked. There was activity on the ground.

I had the feeling I was going for a ride.

## 19

THE GPS TOLD ME TO TURN INTO THE PARKING LOT. THEN IT stopped navigating. "You have reached your destination."

Gasoline saturated the still air. A couple guys dressed in black cargo pants and matching t-shirts stepped out of the shadows. They were armed with assault rifles. They blocked the gate. A third stepped up to the side of the car. I saw him coming but still winced when he slapped the roof.

"You're him?"

I shrugged. "Guess so."

"Got the money?"

I patted the canvas bag.

"Open it," he said.

"Not until I see the girl."

"She's not here."

"Then you're not seeing the money."

The guy stepped back and said something in Greek. The

guard on the left jogged over and took his spot and jammed the muzzle of his rifle against my head. The third guy, still standing at the gate, aimed his weapon in my direction. I flicked the high-beams on. He brought a hand up to shield his eyes.

"You're a fool touching me with that," I said.

The guard said nothing.

"I could disarm you in a second."

The first man leaned in through the passenger side window. "He don't speak English." He grabbed the bag, turned it toward him, unzipped it. Stuck his hand inside and moved the money around. Then he nodded and zipped it up again. He yelled something out. The man at the gate stepped aside, and the gate split in two.

"Go in," the guard said.

I drove in slowly. There were three semi-automatic rifles aimed at the car. Maybe more. I knew from what Esau told me that this operation extended far beyond the six men I had encountered at the cafe.

Another man dressed head to toe in black stepped in front of the car and held out his hand. I pulled to a stop there. Someone yanked my door open and grabbed my shoulder. I jerked away from him and grabbed the cell phone and the canvas bag. One I held in plain sight. The other I tucked in a cargo pocket.

The guy stepped back and had his rifle trained on me as I got out of the car.

Then Chris from the cafe showed up. He was dressed in black as well, wearing a suit. His brown hair was brushed back. He pulled his jacket to the side and showed me his handgun.

"Drop the bag," he said.

"Not until I see the girl," I said.

He took a step back and motioned to one of the guards. The guy came up behind me, kicked my legs to the side and pulled my arms out wide. He ran his hands up and down my body. Reached around the front. Found the gun. Pulled it out. Pushed me away.

I stumbled forward but managed to regain my balance.

The guard walked around me and handed Chris the Beretta.

"What did you need this for?" he said.

"I guess the same reason you need six armed men to deal with me. 'Cause I can't trust you assholes."

Chuckling, he walked toward me. As he drew near, his cologne overpowered the smell of jet fuel. He grabbed my left arm and turned me toward the Gulfstream. The guards formed a loose corridor for us to walk through. At the top of the stairs, standing in the doorway, was Michael. He leaned over the side railing and spit. The wind caught the glob of saliva and it landed dangerously close to us.

"Cut it out," Chris said to him.

Michael shrugged, turned, and went back inside the Gulfstream.

I heard the guards fall in line behind us. Would we all be traveling tonight? Perhaps only a select few would join. I felt they were smart enough to know they wouldn't want to be alone with me in a confined space.

At least the old me, prior to a few months ago.

The current version could go either way.

But on the plane, guns weren't an option. Unless they were fools. But traveling in their boss's multi-million dollar jet would surely add a bit of caution to their actions. No one wanted to be the guy to ground it.

We climbed the stairs and crossed the metal platform. Our

footsteps melded into one and rose into the night. Michael met me at the entrance. He feigned a punch to my gut.

"I said cut it out." Chris sounded agitated. I didn't mind the tension. If the right situation presented itself, I could use it.

Chris shoved me forward and Michael pushed me to the side. Felt like I was in a pinball machine. I grabbed hold of a seat back, swung behind it and planted myself down. The men stared at me, looked at each other, shrugged.

"Sit anywhere you like," Chris said. "Not like you're going anywhere."

"Where're you from?" I asked him, still curious about his neutral accent.

He looked away. Walked past me. Took a seat a few rows back.

"How long is this flight?" I asked.

No one responded.

Two guards climbed on board. They took two seats against the cockpit wall, facing the rest of us. Their gazes remained fixed on me.

The door swung shut. A few silent minutes passed. Air blew from small fans above me. It was piped in and chilled and run through countless filters, distilling it to the point it smelled mechanical. It cooled the sweat on my brow and hairline. Soon after, the roar of the engine overpowered the hiss of the fans. We taxied, slowly at first. The jet built up speed. Forced me back in my seat. The front lifted. The two guards were higher than me. Wind rushed past. Sounded for a moment like the jet was coming apart. The wheels whined and then went silent. The tension eased as we climbed higher into the air.

For a moment I forgot what I was doing there and enjoyed the flight.

That wouldn't last long.

# 20

We never reached a cruising altitude. The jet never leveled out. There was no in flight movie or meal or snack. No flight attendants to bring us drinks. We peaked somewhere around five thousand feet over the sea and then began our descent.

The men facing me got bored of looking at my face and now stared out at the blackness, one looking left, the other right. I had no idea what the guys behind me were doing. I never looked back. Felt drawing attention during the flight was a bad idea. They were couriers. Gophers. I'd see the man I had to deal with soon enough.

Looking out the window, I saw city lights in the far distance, twinkling like miniatures on a train table in the dark. The jet banked away from them and the view faded to black again. A few minutes later, another splash of white lit up the dark countryside. Two long lines of lights, one east to west and the other north to south.

Runways.

The pilot looped around a couple times then made the final approach. It was like take off in reverse. The roar built as the flaps cut into the air. The plane dropped. The landing gear banged then whined as it was lowered. The wind thundered like a pride of lions. The plane bounced and screeched as it touched down, rapidly declining in speed. We slowed to a crawl near the end of the runway.

The jet taxied for a couple minutes before stopping. First the guards facing me rose. One opened the door. The other aimed his rifle at me. The men behind me got up. Michael exited without looking at me. Had to get his brownie points, I supposed.

"Get up," Chris said. He stood a couple feet behind me. Close enough for me to do something to him. But was I far enough from the guard? Did it matter? I was trapped in the jet and I was unarmed. They'd get me sooner or later.

So I rose and clutched the canvas bag like it held everything I cherished in life inside of it. Chris shoved me in the back, and I started walking toward the exit. Men were talking outside. Shouting. Calling out. I heard engines roaring to life. The stale air of the cabin gave way to the salty humid air of the evening. No one waited on the platform. They had gone to the bottom of the stairs. Michael waited there with three guards flanking him. I descended before Chris had a chance to shove me down. My footsteps echoed off the metal stairs. The railing was slick, like it had been washed before the steps were driven over.

The men at the bottom led me to a waiting sedan. It was long and black and the windows were tinted as dark as the night sky. They opened the back door. I climbed in one side.

Chris on the other. They closed his door. Not mine. Chris looked past me and nodded.

"Sorry to do this," he said.

A guard reached in with a black scarf.

"No you're not," I said.

"You're right." He smiled grimly. "Can't have you knowing where we're going, though."

The guard wrapped the cloth around my head multiple times, covering my eyes. He adjusted it, then cinched it tight.

"So I'm getting out of there alive?" I said.

"How should I know? I have no clue what he's going to do with you."

Being unable to place his accent drove me crazy. Where was he from?

All four doors slammed shut. The driver dropped the shifter into gear and revved the engine. We lurched forward. I held onto the bag with both hands as my body tumbled back and left against the door.

We drove for twenty minutes, give or take. I lost track of time in the blackness. I was unable to focus on a single thing. My mind hopped between the past and the present, settling on nothing. I had hoped by this point I'd have a script down, ready with alternatives should something come up that I wasn't prepared for. But the words never came. I'd have to wing it.

The car slowed to a stop. The men up front said something in Greek. I heard the sound of metal grating on metal interspersed with a clicking sound, like a chain on gears. The car pulled forward. The scarf was yanked off my head. I blinked a few times to adjust to the bright light shining in through the windows. We drove in an arc and pulled up next to a black SUV. The engine went silent.

"Wait." Chris opened his door and stepped out. On my side were two men, dressed in black cargo pants and black t-shirts. They held rifles aimed at me.

*No originality,* I thought.

Chris looped around the back of the car and opened my door. One of the guards stood to his side and poked his rifle inside.

Chris said, "Get out."

I obliged. My feet hit hard ground. The surface was loose, though, and one foot slid out a couple inches. I reached up with my left hand, grabbed the frame, and pulled myself out. I looked over the back of the car. The lights cast a glow for twenty feet then gave way to pitch black. In front, I saw a square structure. Stucco covering the walls. A door in the middle. A window on either side, blackened except for a knife of light down the middle where the curtains met. Light seeped out along the edges of the doorframe. There was a fragrance about the air. Almost perfume-like.

Lavender.

I looked for Isadora. Didn't see her. As I was guided toward the door, I spotted the plants along the walk. Long stems and muted purple flowers.

The door opened and I was shoved into a square room that comprised the entire house. Four walls, a door on the opposite side. Stained glass lamps in each corner. An odd dark-blue shag carpet covered the floor. There were four couches, upholstered in velvet. One on the left, and right. Two against the back wall separated by the door. Two to four women sat or lay on each couch. None were completely clothed. At most, they had on a bra and panties. A few had one or the other. A couple were nude.

"The hell goes on here?" I said.

"Just move," Chris said.

I crossed the room. Every woman in there stared at me, smiling, gesturing with some body part, inviting me to visit with them for the night. Or part of it, I supposed.

"Now I know why you blindfolded me," I said. "Trying to keep this all to yourself."

Chris shoved me again.

The back door opened outward before I reached it. There were a few men standing there. They backed away as I neared the opening. A covered walkway lit with string lights stretched out from the door. It curved to the right and disappeared behind the landscaping.

"We can spend a few more minutes inside," I said. "Bag's loaded with cash."

"Shut up, wise ass," Chris said.

"Suit yourself." All I wanted was to plant the idea in his mind. Get him thinking about the women. Get him talking. Maybe break that fake neutral accent he maintained. Was it possible? I had no idea. But I was sore and weak and not up for a fight against a house full of armed men. Any advantage I could gain was welcomed.

A guard jumped out in front of me and led the way. Chris stayed next to me. Like a running back streaking down the sideline, I shifted the bag to the other arm, keeping it on the outside. Not that it mattered. We were here now. If he wanted to pry it from my hands, he would have. He didn't because he knew it would be pointless. When the time came, I'd be a good little errand boy and hand it over.

It wouldn't go quite like that, though.

## 21

THE WALKWAY CURVED A COUPLE TIMES. IT WAS SURROUNDED ON both sides by high hedges that partially blocked the breeze. Though the night air was cool, humidity saturated it. The smells alternated between cheap cologne, body odor, flowers, and lavender. At some point it would be Isadora and not the herb.

We reached another building. Chris grabbed my arm and we stopped. The guard ahead of us went to the door, stopped, and leaned to his side, covering the security panel. I couldn't tell if he entered a code or used an access card, but the lock disengaged with a click that was audible from twenty feet away. The sentry stepped to the side and allowed me into a narrow hallway wide enough for one guy at a time. The corridor stretched thirty feet or so. It was solid, no visible doors or arteries intersecting it.

"Which way?" I said.

"You really don't want to get out of here do you?" Chris said.

"After seeing all those women?"

"I mean alive, asshole."

"You never answered my question."

"Which one?"

"Where are you from?"

"None of your business."

"I can't place your accent."

"Because I worked hard at neutralizing it. Anywhere, Europe. That's where I'm from."

Hardly enough to build a profile on.

He tugged at the bag. I spun and pulled away and had my arm cocked.

"I know I only have a few more minutes with it," I said, "but I'll be the one delivering it. You try that again and I'm gonna turn that pretty little nose of yours into something matching your partner's. Got it?"

The guy smiled wide. "I can get to you, can't I?"

He was playing the same game I was. Only he did it better. The staring competition lasted all of five seconds. He smiled. I forced myself to do the same. Getting out meant going through him in some way or another. *Don't let him in,* I told myself.

The door at the other end opened. A bald guy with a fat head adorned with a salt-and-pepper mustache leaned out. He said something in Greek and motioned us forward.

"After you," Chris said.

I gripped the bag tight, turned, headed to the door. The bald guy took a step back, widening the opening. The room revealed itself a foot at a time. It was dim. The walls were dark wood paneling. The desk was overbearing and solid mahogany. Behind it, built-ins were lined with books. I caught a whiff of pipe tobacco, something similar to what my grandfather smoked in his favorite chair when I was a kid. An old guy stood, facing away. He was shuffling through a section of leather bound tomes.

"Boss," Chris said. "He's here with the money."

The old guy already knew that, though. He took his time tracing each book's spine with his finger, muttering something to himself.

I stood a foot inside the room, surrounded by five guys and couldn't see anything to the left or right. But I knew Isadora was in there. Even amid the musky smell of the men, the lavender stood out.

The old guy pulled down a thick book and turned with it tucked under his arm. He adjusted his glasses as he made eye contact with me. He gave me a slight nod. I didn't reciprocate. An upturned smile formed on his lips. It was Kostas. He looked younger and thinner than Esau, although I knew he was older. It was obvious he kept himself in shape. His clothes were casual, but expensive looking. So were his shoes. Leather with thick soles, they probably cost more than his outfit. He set the book down and opened it to the middle. The pages were curled and brown. The top one lifted an inch or so. Underneath it looked black. He stared down at it.

"Name?" Kostas asked.

"Jack."

"Jack what?"

I looked at Chris. My community was tight. There were people around the world who'd heard my name at one time or another. So I wanted to catch his reaction. He made no move either way when I answered.

"Noble," I said.

"Fitting you show up in that coward Esau's place then," Kostas said.

"The way it was presented, I had no choice."

"Everyone has a choice, Jack Noble. Don't forget that." He straightened and crossed his arms. "You could have easily said no. After all, other than being a resident of the cafe, you have no stake in this. Why risk your neck for him?"

I craned my neck and caught sight of Isadora's exposed leg. It was smooth and shiny with oil. "It's not for him."

Kostas turned his head toward her. Smiled. Nodded. "I see."

I don't know why I exposed myself in that way. He had no leverage on me other than the threat of pain or death. I'd just handed him everything he needed to get me to cooperate. After all, I'd shown up with a paltry twenty thousand dollars. A fifth of what Esau originally owed. A lot less than what the old guy now demanded.

He pointed at the bag. "It's all there?"

The guards stepped back and away from me. Only Chris remained. He put a hand on my back and shoved me forward. I resisted and threw an elbow his way and caught him on the arm.

"That's enough," Kostas said, both hands extended away from his body. "Let me have the bag."

I crossed the room and set the bag on the desk, the zipper fly nearest me. The bag sent a puff of wind out in all directions. The loose page on the book rose and teetered and fell backward, exposing the next page. Only it wasn't a page at all. The book had been hollowed out into a secret compartment, which held a gun. A small silver thing chambered maybe for a .22 caliber bullet.

I glanced up and saw the old guy smiling. What did it

matter? The place was full of armed men. Any one of them could kill me with a single shot.

Unless the guy had other plans. With a .22 he could inflict a lot of pain without causing a mortal wound. I followed his gaze from me, to the gun, then across the room to where Isadora was.

She sat on the couch, legs outstretched, wearing blue running shorts and a white t-shirt with no bra underneath. A book was open on her lap. The title was in Greek. She had a scratch on her cheek like a road burn. Like she'd been shoved to the ground in that cellar and her face took the brunt of the fall. But she'd cleaned up since. Her face was expressionless. Her eyes met mine, and she blinked a couple times. She looked away, first at the old guy, then at nothing. Was she in shock over the whole thing? Had they made threats to her? Did she know I was a dead man walking?

*Dead in Greece.*

When no one other than Frank and Alik knew I was there. The old guy would have Alik taken care of. No doubt about that. And Frank would never tell anyone what had happened. The world was convinced I had already died in Black Dolphin. Why reveal the truth? Why mention the cover up? Hell, Frank would probably dance on my unmarked grave, happy to be done with me.

Kostas glared at me as he grabbed the bag and spun it on the table. It hit the book and knocked it off kilter. I watched as his spotted hand latched onto the zipper and slid it along the track. He peeled the sides of the bag open and reached in with both hands like he was freeing a breached calf. He pulled out a couple bricks of bills, set them on the table. Reached for a couple more while glancing at the top of the stacks. The next stack looked the same, as did the one following that.

He looked up at me again, squinted.

I remained motionless.

He peeled the rubber bands off the bricks and slid the first few bills off. Then he picked up a stack and fanned it. His gaze shifted up as he performed mental calculations. He dug back into the bag again, pulling the bricks out at a furious pace. When all was said and done, half his desk was covered. He flipped each over so the top bill was facing up. Then he pulled the rubber bands off a few others. Peeled the first few bills back. Fanned a few more stacks.

Sweat formed on my brow. I used my thumb like a wiper blade and moved it into my hair.

The old guy looked at the money, then at me, then at the guy next to me. He opened his mouth, said nothing. Looked at the money again. Then at me. Then at the guy next to me.

"Take him out in the hallway. I want a guard at each door. Rest of you, help me count."

Chris grabbed me by the collar and yanked back. I didn't lose my balance. Instead I ducked and freed myself from his grasp and turned to the door.

"You'd better hope it's all here, Jack Noble."

## 22

---

THERE WAS NO CIRCULATION IN THE HALLWAY WHEN THE DOORS at either end were both closed. The floor and ceiling were void of vents. The smell of mold saturated the air. I looked up and saw water damage along the edge of the ceiling on both sides. The carpet below my feet was thick and would soak dripping water right up, creating a breeding ground.

Chris sniffed and wiped his nose.

"Allergic?" I said.

"Shut up," he said.

"Why aren't you in there counting the money?"

He said nothing.

"I mean, seems like an important job. He doesn't trust you?"

"Maybe your life is more valuable to him." He paused a beat. "Don't know why, though. You don't seem to care about it."

"How so?"

"First, you get in the middle of my guys when they're working."

"Didn't like the way they looked."

"Then you do it again."

"If anything, I'm consistent."

"Then you come out here."

"Y'all asked nicely."

"And you do it with way less money than you were supposed to bring."

"I'm broke."

The last part was a lie. But I figured by now, Frank had the majority of my assets frozen so that no one could access them. Not even me. But I always had a backup plan.

"You're stupid," the guy said. "He's going to string you up by your nuts."

"Sounds painful."

"Then take target practice at you with that fancy pistol of his."

"Do I get to spend the night with a couple of those girls out front first?"

"Are you really this arrogant?" Chris said. "I mean, you're facing certain death and all you can do is think with your dick?"

His was exposed to me. Guard down. The sentries were positioned at either end of the hall. We were in the middle. I could take him out. Break his neck right there. They wouldn't reach me in time.

But they would reach me.

And then it'd be over. I'd be shot or beaten, and certainly killed at some point. Isadora would remain the old guy's *guest* for however much longer. I guess until he decided to kill her too. Or drug her up and make her part of his crew in the front house.

The guy smiled at me like he knew what I was thinking. He

even tucked his hands behind his back and turned his face to offer me a better shot. I could see it in his eyes. *Do it*, he was saying. *Take that first shot.*

He had as much confidence as I did. But he wasn't hurt or wounded or in danger of being strung up by his testicles and used for target practice. That bolstered his thoughts of himself.

The door to the room opened. Kostas stood there, silhouetted by the dim light.

"Get in here," he said, turning toward his desk.

Chris extended his arm. The bald guard with the thick head and mustache held the door for me. By the time I entered, Kostas was behind his desk. But I wasn't paying attention to him.

Isadora took one look at me then turned her head. I couldn't tell if she was crying or not.

"Sit," the old guy said.

I remained in place.

He shifted his glance to my right and nodded. A second later, my right leg was swept forward and a heavy set of hands slammed into my chest. I tried to twist and extend my arms to break my fall. Didn't happen. I landed on my left side. The fall was hard, but the carpet was thick and soft and it almost felt like landing on a wrestling mat. Still, the jarring slam left me slightly winded.

Someone grabbed me by the hair and the back of my collar and dragged me up. They tossed me toward a chair. I hit the back of it with my face and it toppled over and so did I. This time the corner of the seat caught me just above the gut on one of my bruised or broken ribs.

The guy righted the chair and pulled me up and sat me in it. I fought to show no reaction to the pain in my midsection.

Couldn't. I leaned forward, to the side, hand on my ribcage. My breathing was rapid and shallow.

"Did you really think you could come in here with less than a quarter of the original debt and walk out alive?" Kostas said.

I felt a buzzing against my thigh. Heard it, too. The old guy glanced at my pocket, then back at me.

"What is that?" he said.

I shrugged.

He glanced to the side and made a motion with two fingers. Four hands descended on me. Yanked me up. Pulled my arms back. Someone went through my pockets. They reached into the cargo pocket and pulled out the cell phone.

The guy stepped into my field of view. The bald guy with the mustache. He set the phone on the desk. The old guy picked it up and stared at it for a moment. Then he set it to the side like it didn't matter. Like someone couldn't use it to track my location.

At least, they could do something like that in the States. I had no idea about here. Even if Alik could pull it off, what were the chances he would have managed a flight over so quickly? I was alone. Isolated. On my own.

"Where is the rest of the money?" the old guy said.

"That's all he's got," I said.

"You know what this means?"

"That was the original deal, right? Twenty grand on a set schedule."

"He missed too many payments on that schedule."

"The guy lost his wife. And he's your friend. Old friend, been through a lot together. He's entitled to a little leeway, right? I mean, damn, he's giving up what he's got left."

Someone behind me cleared their throat. Soft and gentle.

Almost missed it. Isadora. Had it been one of the guys it would have cut through the moment of silence like thunder.

Kostas shook his head slowly, smiling. "You sit there so smug. Think you know everything."

"What don't I know?"

"The only thing you don't know that matters is that Esau sold you out. He set you up. Sure, you might pull it off. Or you might die. Doesn't matter to him."

"It's all he's got."

"He's got the house. The cafe."

"You want those?"

The old guy sat in his chair and leaned back like he was thinking about it. A couple times he asked himself, "Do I want those?"

The atmosphere in the room was heavy. Big shadows moved through the light wash. The door opened. I couldn't tell if people shuffled in and stopped by the doorway, or if they shuffled out. All that was left was the sound of our breathing. The stink of the men. The fragrance of Isadora's hair.

I tensed my abdominal muscles, clenching hard. The pain was manageable. I looked over at Isadora. She stared at me. No tears. No smile. No look of hope. It was as though she thought my being there was a hopeless cause. I was starting to agree. Going in with a fraction of the money was stupid.

The old guy leaned forward. He spun the book with the cutout and the .22 around in a half-circle then stopped it. With his thumb he fanned through the pages front to back, then in reverse. He placed his left palm on the stack of parchment. Retrieved the pistol.

"What assurances do I have he'd hand them over?" Kostas said.

"His word, I guess," I said.

"His word means shit to me," he said.

"That's between the two of you," I said.

"Besides, he doesn't own the house free and clear. Hardly any equity built up."

"The cafe does good business."

"I suppose it does, but maybe that's because of him."

"Maybe it's because of her." I jutted my chin over my shoulder toward Isadora. "The old guys that come in seem to like her."

"She doesn't want to be there, though."

"How would you know?"

The old guy stared at the silver pistol, turning it over in his hand. He looked at it like it was the first breast he'd ever touched. "What would you say the place makes in a day?"

"Me? How would I know?"

"You've been there, what, a month now?"

"Suppose so."

"Well, you have eyes. You see the customers. How much?"

"Like you said, he hasn't made a dent in his house note. My guess is not that much."

The old guy looked up as he shifted the pistol in his palm and gripped the handle and threaded his finger through the trigger guard. He pointed it in my direction without actually aiming it at me.

"Not doing yourself any favors, Jack Noble."

"What do you want me to tell you? The place makes a grand a day? Take it off his hands and you'll be paid back in no time at all?"

His face folded into a thousand crinkles as he smiled. "What did Esau think would happen?"

"He didn't."

"Come again?"

"I said he didn't. He didn't think anything would happen. I made him do this based on what he had told me about you two growing up together and going to war. You see, we're not all that different. I'm a soldier, too. I've been through a lot with a couple partners. One is like a brother to me. The other, not so much. Despite that, I'd die for either, even though one would be happy to set me up under the right circumstances."

"What's this have to do with me and Esau?"

"You were brothers growing up. He lied to join you in the war so you'd have someone always watching your back. That kind of relationship persists no matter the situation. He's been on hard times. You know that. Hell, that's why he came to you in the first place. You've got twenty grand on your desk. It's all he has. He's giving it to you in good faith. Whatever you want to do after this point is up to you, but I think you need to take it up with him now."

The old guy said nothing. His gaze shifted between me and the money.

I looked at Isadora again. She watched me with the same blank look on her face. Shock, I presumed. The situation had left her rattled. Or maybe they'd already started drugging her. That's one way to deal with a combative hostage.

"Let me leave with the girl and I'll present an offer to him," I said.

"Of what?" Kostas asked.

"The cafe. He'll sign it over to you. It's got built in clientele and is right on the water. Maybe you could use it. You know, filter stuff in."

"Like what?" He lifted a curious eyebrow. "What do you know of my business?"

"Your business is your business. I don't care a thing about it."

He sat back and rubbed his chin with his brown age-spotted hand. The other rested on the desktop next to the pistol. His gaze drifted around the room. It stopped four times. The money. Isadora. Me. Someone behind me. Chris, I assumed. That was it. We were the only people in the room. How many remained in the hallway? Smart money said only those who had to be there. The rest would take the opportunity to wait in the first house until they were needed.

I looked back. Chris leaned against the wall next to the door. Too far away for me to reach without risk of being shot either by him or the old guy. He stared at me. His hand went to his holstered pistol. His head swung side to side, slowly.

The old guy cleared his throat, a raspy, hollow sound. "Tell Esau I'll wipe the slate clean. The interest is forgiven. He has two days to come up with the rest of the original debt."

"If he doesn't?"

"Use your imagination."

"The girl?"

"It's up to her."

I stood and turned toward her. "You ready?"

She looked away from me. Didn't get up.

"Isadora?" I said. "Come on, let's get out of here."

Her eyes were closed. She shook her head.

"What are you doing?" I said.

"Sounds like she doesn't want to go," the old guy said. "Chris, escort Mr. Noble out."

The guy approached me slowly and cautiously. He reached out for my arm. I fended off his hand and took a step back.

"Isadora," I said. "What the hell is going on here? Why don't you want to go?"

She opened her mouth, but after casting a glance toward Kostas, closed it. I turned to face him.

"What did you do to her? What's she on?"

"On?"

"You drugged her," I said. "With what?"

"Drugged her?"

"No way she's acting like this on her own."

"Like I said, the choice is hers. She's not being held here against her will."

"What?"

"Never has been."

"We went to the old house. Found her torn clothes. Hell, I can see the scrape on her face from where you assholes threw her on the ground."

The old guy laughed.

"They took her at gunpoint," I said.

"All with her knowledge." He leaned back, smiling. His pistol was within reach. He must've seen me look at it. "Go ahead and try. I may be old, and true I'm a bit slow now. But I'm not that slow. And neither is Chris."

I turned and walked over to Isadora and bent down. "What is he talking about?"

Her eyes were wet and red. She smelled fresh. She shifted, pulling the white shirt tight against her breasts, revealing the outline of her dark nipples. She said nothing.

"Is it true?" I asked. "You knew about all of this?"

"Sort of," she said. "I knew why they were coming."

"And she agreed to be taken," the old guy said.

"What?" I said. "Why?"

"He has the money, Jack. Uncle Esau has it. Maybe not at the cafe or the house, but he has it."

"How do you know this?"

"Because he never used it."

"What do you mean he never used it?"

"My aunt never had the surgery."

## 23

I ROCKED BACK ON MY HEELS AFTER HEARING THE CONFESSION. Esau had come across as a man devastated. He'd lost everything, including his wife, and in the process had taken on a loan greater than he could handle from a criminal. And now Isadora was saying some of it was a lie.

I took a deep breath, inhaling her lavender scent. Tears spilled over and dripped down the sides of her soft cheeks. A couple drops fell on my hand. Her hair splayed over the pillows and her shoulders. A synapse fired deep in my brain and I wished we were alone somewhere far from this mess. I realized what it was about her. She was the kind of woman who made any situation so light it floated away like a balloon.

"How do you know this?" I asked her.

She licked her lips and cleared her throat. "After they started harassing my uncle, I started digging around his paperwork. He wouldn't come right out and tell me what had happened, so I really had no choice. I found all the doctor and hospital receipts. But never anything for the operation. I even called the doctor, posing as my mother. They were confounded by my request. There had been no surgery. But he had a pamphlet on it, with what I thought were dates and times scribbled on it."

I recalled the paper Alik and I had found in the cellar of the abandoned house.

"How did he pull it off?" I said. "How did he make you believe she had the surgery?"

"She was in bad shape by that point. She didn't know what was going on. He sent her away for a little bit. Told us the doctor said no one could see her. I don't think she was ever coherent again. It wasn't long after that she passed. But I'd look at her, and say something about the procedure, and she'd get this confused look."

"This doesn't make any sense. Where's the money then?"

She shrugged. "I don't know. He's hiding it somewhere. And I want him to pay it back. I want him to pay it back with interest, because he hurt my mother, and he stole my life from me. If my aunt had had the operation, I might have been able to leave and continue with my education. Instead, I wept for my aunt, for my tortured mother, and for my distraught uncle. And I stayed. The old bastard duped everyone. He robbed me of my future, Jack."

I glanced back at the old guy. He sat stoic, said nothing, made no movement or gesture.

Isadora said, "I don't want to see him again. I don't want to go back there. They are treating me well here." She nodded at Kostas. "Uncle Esau needs to repay his debt. I'll wait here until you return with the rest of the money."

I leaned in close to her. Her lips brushed my cheek. I spoke softly. "You don't have to do this. If they're putting you up to this, tell me. I can get you out of here."

"No, Jack," she whispered. "It's all true. Please, just go and get the rest."

I remained there for a moment. Her breath was hot on my neck. Her skin soft against mine. I didn't know what to think. The whole situation had been turned upside down. I needed space and time to work it out. Needed to run it by Alik. Needed to speak to Esau and get the truth from him.

"Two days, Jack Noble," the Kostas said.

"What if he doesn't have it?" I said.

"He'd better."

"And if he doesn't? Will you take the cafe?"

"We already worked it out that the place doesn't earn anything. Why would I want it?"

"It's something, at least."

"He has two days to come up with the money."

The old guy's stare shifted to the door. I heard it open. Looked back. Chris had left his position and someone else took it. He walked over to where Isadora sat. Stopped behind her. Pulled out his pistol and aimed it at the top of her head.

She gasped and sunk into the couch. The guy yanked her back up by a fistful of hair.

"Use your imagination, Jack Noble," the old guy said.

I crossed the room, stopped at the door, looked back at Isadora. "Should've left and given me your monologue on the plane."

## 24

A GROUP OF MEN USHERED ME DOWN THE HALLWAY, ALONG THE outside walkway, and into the square room with the women. About half were still there. None were nude. Maybe I had come through at shift change. Maybe they were hired only for the night. A celebration? Three guys sat with six women on two couches. Everyone looked at me.

"Wait here," the bald guy with the fat head and mustache said.

He bumped into me as he passed on his way to the front door. One of the women smiled at me. I looked away from her. The door opened up. The car sat outside.

"OK," the bald guy said. "Let's go."

They escorted me outside. One guy sat up front. The bald guy in back with me.

"We'll have no problems, right?" he said.

I shrugged, said nothing.

"I'd feel better if you agreed with me," he said.

"I'd feel better if I had the girl with me," I said.

"You want a woman?" He lifted an eyebrow and smiled. "I
ı go back inside and get you one."

' looked away. "We'll have no problems. Now let's go."

The drive was quicker going back. Less than ten minutes
had passed when I first spotted the lights of the airport. Either
they'd driven in circles on the way to the house, or time slowed
down with the blindfold on. I wasn't sure why they hadn't put it
back on now. I figured the guy wasn't used to doing this and
had screwed up.

So I spent the entire drive remembering every landmark we
passed while looking like I was doing nothing but nodding off
to sleep.

The jet remained on the apron where we'd left it. The driver
pulled up next to it. The front door opened. The guy walked
around the back of the car, opened my door.

"Get out," the bald guy with the mustache said.

"What about you?"

He shook his head. "Only you. Get on the plane. We're
gonna wait right here and watch and make sure you are on
board when it lifts off."

"And if I don't get on?"

He pulled back his coat and grabbed the handle of his pistol.

I looked up at his smiling face. "You know you wouldn't get
that out before I hit you."

"You want to try it? Be my guest."

I heard the guy behind me back up and rack the slide of his
pistol. The sound came from three or four feet away. Even if I
did get to the bald guy in time, I'd still get shot.

"Well?" he said.

"You'd better hope you're not at the house next time I'm

there." I swung my leg and planted it on the ground. Heard the other door open. When I stood, he was watching me from over the roof.

"You don't want there to be a next time," he said. "A next time means the end of your life. Now get on that plane."

A surge of anger rose up like bitter bile in my throat. I forced it down. Nothing good could come from getting into a fight out here. Not when I had two armed men who remained out of arm's reach.

A second car pulled in. Headlights washed over the tarmac. Doors opened. Two other guys got out. Two silhouettes approached me. I figured they were joining me on the flight.

Chris walked right up to me. He reached into his pocket. I tightened my chest and arms to ready them for action. He pulled out a folded piece of paper and held it between us.

"For Esau," he said. "Make sure he gets it."

I took it from him and slipped it in my pocket. Thought about what it might be. A finger? Wasn't thick enough. And there was no lump. Maybe a lock of hair.

"A revised contract," he said. Then he smiled. "Written in the woman's blood."

Something happened in my brain and signals traveled along synapses then down my nerves and reached my arms and the muscles fired on their own. My left hand rose up in a defensive position while the right drove forward a distance less than a foot. But the distance didn't matter because my fist was a like an engine revved to the red line and suddenly thrown into gear. It plowed forward hard and fast while the fingers curled and rose and my palm drove into the guy's solar plexus.

It happened so fast he didn't have time to deflect the blow or prepare his abdominal muscles for the strike.

He expelled all the air in his lungs and his shoulders hunched forward while his back bowed. A flurry of movement occurred around me as three men pulled their weapons and started shouting in as many languages. Chris dropped to his knees. He had one arm wrapped around his stomach and the other planted on the ground for support. He was desperately trying to suck in a mouthful of air. All that happened was he made a gritty hollow type sound and his face turned red in the false light.

The metal stairs and deck next to the jet clanged as it filled with the pilot and the rest of the flight crew. They watched on with open mouths and spoke in hushed tones.

The bald guy started shouting at me. The other two joined in. They drew closer to me. I couldn't see all three at once. I stepped back and turned in a quarter-circle.

"Enough," Chris shouted. He cradled his gut with one hand and lifted the other. He swayed on his knees, then lifted one and got a foot planted on the ground. "No one harms him. He gets on the plane. Those are orders. Got it?"

No one moved. Someone coughed from the platform. They followed it up with something in Greek. Sounded timid.

"Got it?" the guy shouted.

Three sets of hard-soled shoes backed away from me. I looked around and saw three weapons holstered. Another chance to do something. Not enough of one. As soon as I secured a weapon, the others would be raining bullets on me, orders or not.

"Now get on the damn plane, Jack, and hope that you never encounter me again."

# 25

_____

As I climbed the stairs, the breeze grew stiffer. Still smelled of oil and gas and rubber, as though I stood in a mechanic's garage. The railing felt cool and slick. Half the flight crew boarded before me. The other half followed me in. My escorts remained on the ground. I took a seat on the side of the plane nearest them and stared out the window. One by one, they broke off their gaze and returned to their respective vehicle. Chris remained until the end. He watched me while the jet taxied and was still standing there when we barreled down the runway, his black suit flapping.

Like the drive to the small airport, the flight back was shorter. I figured that was something out of Kosta's control. Not much was, it seemed. Even had me under it.

To a point, at least.

I'd hand over the letter and I'd make Esau tell me where the rest of the money was hidden. I'd arrange the drop and even bring the money if I had to, so long as it was public. No way in hell was I going back to the house. They could threaten me with anything they wanted and I wouldn't step foot in there again.

I wondered if Alik could arrange someplace else for us to stay. Would Frank go for it? Would he send some help to deal with the mess, or apply pressure to Kostas? He was one of Greece's top criminals. Surely he didn't want the SIS or CIA looking into his dealings. Likewise, Kostas presumably had contacts within the Greek government and potentially in intelligence. That caused all sorts of problems. The kind of problems Frank wouldn't want to deal with.

The jet crested, hung there for a moment, and then began its descent. The airstrip was in view. The pilot banked left, looped around, then dropped the bird down and landed.

A woman came out and opened the door. She looked at me, smiled, turned, disappeared into the cockpit. They wanted nothing to do with me. I was surprised they hadn't locked the doors after what had happened on the ground. They must've been on the old guy's payroll. Only explanation.

I rose and made my way to the door, passing bursts of stale air from the overhead vents, happy to get out. At the opening I swept my gaze across the lighted tarmac. At the edge of the wash I saw a familiar sight. Esau's car. Alik stepped forward. Both hands were out of view. Both held a weapon, I presumed. He nodded. I returned the gesture, then I exited and climbed down the stairs. The whine of the jet engine blocked out all other sounds. Alik turned his head left and right and looked over his shoulders. Even when his head didn't move, his eyes darted around.

Ten feet away, I said, "Relax, it's only me. Everyone else stayed behind."

It didn't calm him.

"How'd you know I'd be here?" I said.

"They called with the phone you brought," Alik said.

He'd left the car running. We got inside. He shifted into gear before I had my door shut.

"They say anything worth mentioning?" I said.

Alik shrugged. "Just that you were on a plane and where and when to pick you up. Said I had better be there on time because they had snipers on the ground and if you stood there for five minutes they'd blow your head off."

Now I understood his apprehension. He hadn't been afraid of anyone on the plane. I glanced around, wondering whether it was true or if they were trying to get a rise out of us.

"Bullshit," I said. "Where are they hiding?"

"Don't know. Don't care." He turned onto the road and slammed the gas to the floor. The cabin darkened and filled with diesel fumes. I lowered my window an inch. The wind roared in and out and neutralized the air.

"Did you tell Esau?" I said.

"No," he said.

"Care to know what happened?"

"Not really."

"I need to talk to someone about it."

"Call them when we get back to the apartment."

"Dammit, Alik. This isn't over. And until it's over, we aren't safe in the apartment. So either get Frank on the phone and tell him we need to move or cooperate and listen to me."

He clutched the steering wheel with both hands while glancing between the road and me. He jerked to the right and we slid to a stop on the gravely shoulder.

"So tell me then," Alik said.

He faced me while I told him what had happened at the

house, starting with the blindfolded ride, and all the way up to punching Chris and no one doing anything about it.

"So they think you can deliver?" Alik said.

I shrugged. "Guess they're thinking I can. The money has to be somewhere, right? If Esau doesn't come up with it, he's a dead man. And Isadora won't leave the house alive. They made that clear."

"You want me to call Frank? Get us out of here?"

I sat for a long moment, staring out into the blackness. Part of me agreed that getting Frank involved was the best option. He could move us. Maybe I could convince him to send some muscle over to help free Isadora. Chances of that were slim, though. Frank was under intense scrutiny lately. Always being watched by someone in the Pentagon. They'd see the movement no matter how hard he tried to hide it. Would only be a matter of time before they tracked it back to me.

"Frank's out," I said.

"Why?"

"Only thing he can do is get us off the island."

"How is that a bad thing?"

"I know you compartmentalize well, Alik. I do most of the time, too. But this isn't part of the job. It's become personal."

He shifted into gear and started the car rolling forward again. "I guess it's time to shake down Esau then."

## 26

ALL THE LIGHTS WERE ON INSIDE THE CAFE WHEN WE PULLED UP to the curb. Someone had placed a large piece of plywood over the shattered window. Perhaps they were there now making the repair. I scanned my surroundings, then jogged over and peered inside. The dining room was empty. A tool bag sat open on a table.

"Let's go around," Alik said.

We went in through the side entrance, walked past the stairs, stepped into the cafe. Esau's door was open. The light was on. He was sitting there tapping on his keyboard. He looked worn down and distraught.

I stepped to the door, knocked on it.

Esau looked up. The monitor splashed blue light over his face. Shadows formed where lines etched his face. The skin under his eyes was dark and puffy.

He got up halfway out of his seat. "Where is she?"

I shook my head as my voice caught in my throat.

Alik spoke for me. "We need to talk with you, Esau."

Settling back into his office chair, he motioned us in. He avoided our stares. Instead, his gaze swept over his desk. He shuffled loose papers from either end into a hectic stack, then picked it up and banged it against his desk until they were as uniform as they were going to get. He spun and placed them on a low shelf, then turned back toward us slowly. His eyes lingered on his monitor, then shifted down toward his keyboard. He straightened it then picked up the mouse and set it next to the number pad.

"Did you see her?" he asked quietly, still avoiding our eyes.

"I did," I said.

"And?"

"She's well. They've treated her fine. She…" I didn't know how much to tell him. Isadora saw nothing wrong with what she had done since it was in response to Esau's transgressions. But Esau would look at it as betrayal. "She had a small scratch on her face. Told me it was from falling because she tripped over her feet."

A slight smile formed on Esau's lips. "She's always been a klutz."

I said nothing. Neither did Alik. We breathed in rhythm, waiting for Esau to build the courage to ask the next question.

After a few minutes, he did. "So, if she's not here, does that mean Kostas rejected my offer?"

I reached into my pocket and pulled out the folded note. Held it up and waved it. "He countered."

Esau reached for the note. I lowered it out of view.

"What?" he said.

"I need you to level with me, Esau."

"What is it?"

"What did you do with the money Kostas gave you?"

"I told you, I paid for my wife's botched surgery."

"Botched?"

"It failed. Didn't work. Wasted all that money and she died anyway."

Alik said, "What really happened?"

Esau said, "What do you mean? I just told you."

"You tried to spoon feed us bullshit."

Esau's face reddened and his eyes opened wide and his nostrils flared out. "What are you saying to me?"

I said, "Just want you to be straight with us, Esau."

The veins on the side of his head and neck stood out. He slammed his hands open-palm on the desktop. The keyboard rattled and the mouse jumped an inch to the right.

"Why don't you just come out and call me a liar?"

For a few moments the only sound in the room was his ragged breath, fast and erratic, drawing in and expelling out.

"You're a liar, Esau," I said.

He lunged forward, but stopped. Whether of his own accord or because his knees hit the desk, I don't know. Slowly he settled into his chair. His hands rose toward his face. He cupped them over his cheeks and eyes. Pulled down with his fingers pressed tight, drawing his lower eyelids down and revealing the pink flesh underneath. His hands slipped further down his cheeks. He tucked his chin to his chest and stared down at the keyboard.

"What do you know?" he asked.

I said, "That your wife never received the operation."

"How do you know this?"

I had to craft my words so that I remained a step ahead. Once I informed him that Isadora told me, he'd question why.

"Your niece found all the paperwork. She called the doctor's office. They told her that your wife never had the surgery."

Esau nodded slowly. Looked up. First at Alik, then me. "And why did she tell you this?"

"I told you Kostas and his men are being good to her, but she's still being held against her will. They had guns on both of us when I handed them a bag that contained a fifth of what you'd borrowed. I knew they weren't going to do anything. She was scared, though. I guess she thought she was buying us time by telling them you never spent the money."

Esau said nothing.

"My question is why didn't she know this from the beginning? She was here, right? She would have known your wife never had the surgery."

Esau shook his head. "We sent her away. I told her Eleni insisted on it. That she didn't want to burden the girl post-op. She said we were bringing in help. So I arranged a month away for Isa. Time to relax and be a young woman. By the time she returned, my wife had slipped so far she didn't talk anymore. I made sure the nurse was always at her side to keep my niece from prying around."

By now he looked like a defeated man. Slumped in his chair. Elbows on the chair arms, supporting his torso. He propped his head up with one hand. Balled the other into a fist.

"So where is it?" Alik said.

Esau said nothing.

"Where are you hiding the rest of the money?" Alik said.

Esau looked away and still said nothing.

Alik stood and leaned over the desk. He grabbed Esau by the

wisps of hair on his head and forced him to look up. "You fool. Your niece is in danger of losing her life. Where are you hiding the fucking money?"

"The money's gone!" Esau shouted. "Gone! I don't have it anymore!"

## 27

ALIK RELEASED THE OLD GUY AND STEPPED BACK, KICKING HIS chair. It tipped over and banged against the wall. He looked down at me, held out his hands, shrugged like he'd been defeated.

I leaned forward and placed my arms on the desk. "Esau? What do you mean the money's gone? What'd you do with it?"

He coughed as he wiped tears from his cheeks and eyes. The redness faded from his skin. "I had a lead. A good one, you see."

"A lead on what?" I said.

"I couldn't lose this time. I'd sat out when so many other opportunities came. But I tracked each one, and they were all winners. I knew that the time was right."

"What are you talking about, old man?" Alik righted his chair and lowered himself onto it.

"The time was right, yes it was." Esau swiveled ninety degrees and pulled open a drawer. He was muttering in Greek as he rifled through it, then another, and finally the bottom one.

He pulled out a slip of paper that looked like it had been folded, dropped in mud, sprayed with water, and trampled on by a pack of wild animals. "Ah, here it is."

"What's that?" I asked.

"I had the money for about a week or two. Eleni didn't know about it. I never told Isadora about it. Not like she knew of our finances anyway. Maybe what her mother had told her, but that information would come from my wife, and she didn't really know *everything*. So I had the money, got the tip, spent a couple thousand to ship Isa off for a month."

Alik and I glanced at each other. Said nothing.

"The day of, I told my wife that I was headed to see a new doctor about a procedure. She wanted to go, of course. But I told her she was too weak. If everything went well, we'd have the doctor come here to take a look at her."

"Day of what?" Alik said.

Esau took a deep breath. His gaze darted between the two of us. He smiled for a couple seconds, wider than I'd ever seen, revealing teeth brown near his red gums.

"I couldn't lose," he said.

"Lose?"

"At the track," Esau said. "It was a sure thing. My source had been right fifty out of fifty times. And this time, it was on a forty to one longshot."

I leaned back in my chair, dumbfounded at what Esau had said. "You bet the money you borrowed for your wife's surgery on a horse?"

He shook his head. "Not just any horse. A true lock to win. At those odds, I couldn't pass it up. It would have solved all our problems."

"How'd that turn out?"

His excitement and his gaze both fell a notch. He lifted his hand and separated his thumb and index finger a couple inches. "Lost by a nose."

"Jesus Christ," I said. "You've gotta be fucking kidding me. I risked my neck and you risked your niece's life over money you lost at the track?"

Esau said nothing, which only served to intensify my anger.

I stood and kicked my chair back and kicked the desk toward him. His knees were underneath, leaving nothing but his arms and chest to stop the desk from colliding with the wall. He flung himself backward, but not in time. The edge smashed into his stomach. He bowed forward with his mouth twisted in a soundless scream.

Alik jumped up and positioned himself between me and Esau. "Not now, Jack. Not like this."

"Like what then?"

Alik pushed me toward the door. I held up my hands in retreat.

"It's OK. I'm cool."

"OK." Alik backed off.

Esau was waving his hands over his head. His face had turned beet red. He'd either get a breath to his lungs, or have a stroke. Couldn't tell which. After a few more seconds, he gulped air in with a horrid sound. He took a few more breaths, each a little less grating than the one prior.

A few more seconds passed and he spoke. "I'm sorry, my friend, but it had to be done."

"How the hell can you rationalize this? Huh? You just a regular degenerate?"

He swung his head side to side. "No, not at all. I had the money Kostas had lent me, but it wasn't enough. It is true that I spoke to that doctor. And I was going to see him. But I asked how much the surgery would cost and I wasn't even close. I thought maybe there'd be help, but it was considered radical and progressive and no one would help fund it. You see, I had no choice."

"The house?" Alik said. "How much equity?"

"I told you before," Esau said. "None."

"And the cafe?"

"A bit, but not enough to pay back the debt. And it doesn't make enough money to tempt Kostas. I tried that before."

I opened the paper Chris had handed me. "The original debt is what he'll take, minus the twenty percent you already paid."

"I don't have it," Esau said. "I don't have that kind of money. What you took was all there was."

I stepped forward. Alik moved to block my path. I held out my arm and nodded at him. "It's OK." Then I looked at Esau. "I don't know what to do for you now. Kostas stated his case clearly. If you don't pay up, then you and Isadora are dead. And I'm guessing he's gonna make you watch her die, and then he'll drag your death out for as long as he can. Old friends or not, he's not someone you mess with."

I spun and left the office. Stepped into the cafe and climbed the stairs. The echoes of Esau's wails followed me to the apartment.

## 28

I STOOD IN FRONT OF THE OPEN WINDOW, STARING OUT AT THE darkness. The waves rolled and crashed and the wind carried the salt spray into the apartment. It pelted my face like tiny raindrops. I closed my eyes and remained there while my thoughts drifted, recalling scenes throughout the past couple days.

Nothing Isadora had said or done had directly implicated her involvement in this. I couldn't find any evidence that she sought Kostas to initiate the downfall of her uncle. But it was clear that she had some idea what they were going to do. Maybe she thought she was helping by telling Kostas what she had discovered. She had pushed back against my help. Every look she had given me said *stay away*. I thought it was because of how weak I was from my recovery. Kostas must have instructed her to keep outside involvement to nothing. Could the reason she was being held be due to my insisting I could help?

I figured Kostas's men saw us snooping around that old

house where we found her blouse. They must've known we'd end up there. Why else stage it the way they had? Made it more convincing, that's for sure. Maybe if we hadn't gone, they'd have told Esau to go out there. Seeing her torn clothing on the cellar floor would have been enough to get him to step it up and deliver on his debt. At least, they could hope so.

The thing that pissed me off was that Isadora had an idea of who Alik and I were. She knew we were the kind of men who could help her. I felt betrayed that she didn't bring us in on what was going on.

I understood her position, though. And I couldn't help but think that there was another reason behind her decision. Something she couldn't say to me while I stood in Kostas's office. Maybe she had some crazy idea planned out. Or perhaps it was something simple.

The door rattled and I opened my eyes and stood in place. The wind rushed in through the temporary tunnel. The sound of the waves grew louder. I licked my lips. Tasted the salt.

"You say anything else to him?" I asked.

"No." Alik crossed the room and stopped next to me. He folded his arms across his chest. He took a few deep breaths, started to speak, stopped.

"What is it?"

"I think I should call Frank."

"No."

"What do you propose then, Jack? We go in there armed with pistols and take on an organized crime boss and all his thugs? Hell, you couldn't stand up to them here in the cafe. Imagine what will happen when we are there and they can use their weapons. We won't get past the front door."

"I know where the place is. I've got an idea of the layout of the property. We can go in under the cover of night. Or in the middle of day. Doesn't make much of a difference to me. I just want to get her out of there."

"And let's say hypothetically that we pull off this mission. What then? What next for Isadora and Esau? My God, Jack, it'll never end. They'll come after them. And they'll come after us. You can forget about our cover, or whatever it is we've got going on here. Kostas will take that security footage and start showing it to his contacts. Won't be long until the wrong people learn our whereabouts. Have you thought about that?"

I stared at the faint whitecaps streaming toward shore and said nothing.

"Have you? Have you considered what would happen if Ivanov learned of our location? Who do you think can have someone here sooner? Frank, or a Russian General?"

"Frank's got contacts everywhere. I've got contacts from the CIA."

He shook his head. "Don't bullshit me. I know all about you. No one in the CIA likes you. You were a pain in the ass when you were attached and you exposed a rogue operative. And even if there was someone out there who thought enough of you to help, all it would take is one look at your file to see all the shit you've done the past five years. They'd sell you out in a heartbeat. They'd just as soon see you die at Ivanov's hand."

"So why are you here?"

He turned to me, arms still crossed, shaking his head. "Right now, I have no idea. And that's why I'm calling Frank."

"And what are you going to tell him?"

"That I'm getting the hell out of here and he can do whatever he wants with you."

"What do you think he's gonna say to that?"

"Fuck what he says. This is my decision."

"You wanna look over your shoulder the rest of your life, waiting for some guy like me to show up?"

Alik said nothing.

"How are you gonna explain this whole mess to him?"

He puffed air out of one side of his mouth in a mock laugh. "That's easy. I will blame it on you."

"You think he's gonna care?"

Alik looked toward the sea and didn't reply.

"You know what he'll do, don't you?"

"Yeah." He paused a beat. "Same thing Kostas will do if we go after him."

"Who'd you rather take your chances with?"

"I don't know, Jack. I just don't know."

"There's another option hiding behind door number three."

Alik's head bobbed back a couple inches. "What? Door what?"

"It's an expression. Just call it option C."

"OK. What is it?"

"I've got the money."

## 29

THE WIND BLEW IN THROUGH THE OPEN WINDOW AND SWIRLED around the living room and kitchen, stirring up loose papers. Clouds bunched together in the distance. They looked bright against the dark sky. The only sound was the rolling and crashing waves.

"What money?" Alik said.

"I've been working as a contractor for a long time," I said. "With a partner, most of the time. We've taken on a lot of high paying jobs. I invested what I made in different opportunities."

"I don't get you. This isn't our problem. It's theirs. Why are you burdening yourself with Esau's mess?"

I shook my head at him. "There's a fundamental difference between us. It's why you're stuck as a yes man—"

"Don't you ever call me that," he said, stepping toward me and reaching out with his hand. "If I were a yes man I wouldn't be here helping you. I risked everything for this. I'm a criminal in my country now."

I hesitated before responding, waiting for him to back off. After a few seconds he did.

"I guess I phrased that wrong," I said. "Regardless of what you're doing for me, you're still acting on orders given by someone else."

"What were you doing when you got into this mess? When you got yourself sent to Black Dolphin?"

"I…" I turned toward the window, dropped my head back and let the wind wash over me and stir up a recent memory. Before that moment, I hadn't realized the similarities. "Christ, I did the same thing before."

"What?"

"Mandy," I said. "The little girl."

"Who?"

"This whole thing started when I stopped to help a girl lost in the city. Turned into this gigantic mess that took me from the States, to Paris, to Italy. I picked up a couple jobs along the way. That's how the Russians got to me. What they didn't realize was how much more there was to it."

"So you see," Alik said. "Your lack of self control is what gets you into these situations."

I said nothing as he walked to the kitchen. He opened the fridge and pulled out two beers. He popped the caps and set one on the counter.

"For you," he said. "Maybe it'll help you think straight."

The bottle felt cold and wet in my hand. I took a long pull of the cold beverage. Tasted better than anything I'd had all day, which hadn't been much. I felt a twinge in my side with each swallow.

"I know we can move on," I said. "Get Frank to relocate us. Explain how we wound up in the middle of something just because we were in the room. And maybe in time I won't care about it anymore. But right now, I can't see it, man. No matter how bad Esau and Isadora screwed up, I have to do this."

Alik lifted his bottle to his mouth.

I said, "You don't have to be a part of it. If you want to, great. If not, I'll be glad to tell Frank that I forced you to stay out of it."

"I don't understand you."

"I don't understand myself. But, you know, these people, they didn't know us, and it was obvious we had trouble on our heels. Despite that, they put us up. They invited us in, full-well knowing they could get caught in the crosshairs."

"A cynic would say they did it because then we would owe them a favor."

"That might be."

Alik shrugged. "Who knows? And I think there is more to this. I think Esau is into something else that he's not telling us. Whether with this Kostas fellow, or someone else."

"That may be, but I don't know it's relevant right now."

"What is then?"

"Isadora. We get her out, then everything falls in line where it needs to."

Alik stood there, beer at his side, shaking his head. He tried to dissuade me for another half hour. Nothing he said changed my mind.

We'd moved to the table. The wind had picked up something fierce, so we closed the windows. It felt hollow in the apartment. Like we sat in a vacuum.

"How's this work?" Alik said. "Won't it give your identity away?"

"It's a Swiss account," I said. "One I used all the time while operating under various identities."

"So you have one specific name you use with the bank?"

"No." I spun a notebook in front of me and sketched out the flow. "I can initiate the transfer from a computer, if necessary. Then at a local bank, there is an access code that the banker relays to the representative in Switzerland. Then I get on the phone and there's a series of questions I have to answer."

"Esau has a computer in the office. Think he's still down there?"

"I say we go find out."

My heart rate increased as we left the apartment. As far as I knew, no one could tell when activity occurred on the account, because no one knew about it. But nothing was certain. I'd have to remain alert when I went in to collect the money.

We headed down the stairs and stepped into the dark cafe. The street lamps outside were off. The only light was that which seeped through the cracks and underneath Esau's office door.

Alik knocked on it.

There was no response.

He reached down and checked the knob. "Locked."

"Esau?" I said. "We need to talk to you."

Still no answer.

"Think he left?" Alik said.

I shrugged. "Doesn't matter, I guess. What we really need is access to the computer. He doesn't strike me as the kind of guy to shut down every night. And if he does, I doubt it's password protected."

"I can get onto it even if it is."

"Then let's get that door open."

"Wait here."

Alik went behind the counter, opened up a drawer. Utensils

clattered against each other as he searched for something. He returned with a thin metal spatula and a butter knife. It took him about fifteen seconds to get the door open.

"Better than forced entry," he said, looking back at me with a smile that faded when he saw the look on my face.

"Jesus," I said.

We tried to enter the room at the same time and collided. I stepped back, let Alik go in first. My hand lingered on the fine grit of painted brick. Blood coated the wall behind where Esau had sat. Lines of it streaked toward the floor. The old guy was slumped forward. His head, at least what remained, rested on top of his desk calendar, surrounded by a pool of blood. The floor must've been tilted, because his blood dripped over the edge, landing on the floor where Alik and I had stood earlier. It continued in a narrowing line toward the middle of the room where it pooled again.

I crossed the room, careful to stay out of the fluid. Next to Esau's head and outstretched arm was his gun. It had chunks of brain and bone and spatters of blood on it. A piece of paper stuck out from under his face. It was handwritten. A pen sat next to it. A note, I supposed. Didn't bother picking it up. Crimson coated the paper, rendering it unreadable.

"Think he did it himself?" Alik said.

"Check your phone," I said. "Any missed calls?"

He pulled the cell from his pocket. "No."

"They'd have said something to us if Kostas arranged this."

Alik nodded, said nothing.

"You dumb son of a bitch," I said to Esau's corpse.

"It had to be the confession," Alik said.

"That's a weight off his shoulders," I said. "Which only made the knowledge that Isadora would die because of him that much more painful. If only he knew, then maybe he'd have made it through the night. But he'd told us his secret."

"Should we call someone?" Alik said.

I shook my head. "We do that, Kostas will find out. Once he does, he's got no more use for Isadora. How long you think he keeps her around?"

Shrugging, he said, "So what do we do?"

"Find a towel. Wipe the door down so your prints aren't on it. There's more plywood in the dining room. We'll cover the front door and the other window with it. People will assume the place is closed for repairs. Once we've finished with Kostas, we'll phone in an anonymous tip."

A few minutes later we exited the cafe through the side door, behind the stairwell. The wind whipped around the buildings, hammering everything in its path.

"Storm coming," Alik said, looking south where the gathering clouds approached. "Might make getting across to the mainland difficult."

I glanced at my watch. It was four a.m. Too early for the ferry. No commercial airport close by was large enough to have flights running at this time. And even if they did, we wouldn't be able to get tickets without proper ID.

So we got in Esau's car and Alik drove until we were out of town. He pulled to the side of the road and retrieved his cell phone.

"What're you doing?" I said.

"I know someone who can get us off the island," he said.

# 30

AN HOUR LATER I SAT IN THE CRAMPED BACKSEAT OF A SMALL Cessna, staring east at the orange horizon. The glow of a sunrise an hour away. I'd never met the man piloting the craft. He didn't offer his name. Neither did Alik. And I didn't ask. He was getting us from point A to B and that was all that mattered.

He said the flight would take about half an hour, so I settled in for the cramped ride and thought through the day. Problem was, I could only envision a small portion of it. We'd find a bank. I'd go in and speak with a banker to initiate the transfer. The process would take thirty minutes max. Then we'd make the call. What happened then was anyone's guess. And there was nothing I could do about it while up in the air, so I closed my eyes and leaned my head back and pretended to sleep.

The small plane bounced on the rough wind currents. I leaned over and looked out the window. Nothing but dark sea below that the morning hue hadn't colored yet.

The pilot smoothed the plane out again. I closed my eyes once more and managed to drift off.

The sky was a bit brighter when the sound of the landing gear scratching the runway woke me. The pilot hit the brakes and the little Cessna jerked to a stop, whipping my head forward.

Alik looked back and pointed at a waiting taxi and then stuck his thumb in the air. I grabbed the pilot's shoulder and squeezed a thank you.

I swept the tiny airport with my gaze before I stepped foot on the ground. It didn't look like the place I'd been the day before.

Before leaving, we consulted a map. I pointed at the location of the house. The pilot pointed at a nearby town with a bank large enough to accommodate my request. So I assumed the airstrip was somewhere in between.

Alik rushed ahead to the taxi. He climbed in front, perhaps vetting the driver. Our plans were unknown to anyone. We hoped. It'd crossed my mind a couple times that perhaps Kostas had managed to hack the phone and turn it into a microphone. I know I'd gone into a room with a cell set up like that before. But even if they had, they wouldn't know where we were. It would be a waste of manpower to put a man in every cab in the area, or to try and locate every cab.

I opened the rear passenger door and slid in on the vinyl bench seat. Stretched my leg out across it. Leaned against the door. Up front, Alik and the driver were speaking in Greek. Alik twisted in his seat and told me we had a half hour drive, and another hour after that for the bank to open.

So I closed my eyes and drifted off again as the cab bounced along old country roads.

When I awakened this time we were in a parking lot behind a three story industrial looking building. Smoke stacks rose and the wind blew the wisps until they disappeared amid the grey sky. Men of varying ages and sizes, but all dressed the same, strolled down the sidewalk carrying backpacks or lunch bags. Most veered off at some point along the way. Only a few continued on past the building.

"This the bank?" I said.

"No," Alik said. "He agreed to wait with us until it opens. Then he's going to stick with us after."

"I don't know about that," I said.

The guy looked up at the rearview and met my stare. The sparse grey hairs on his lip spread as he smiled. He said something in Greek, which sounded like a greeting I'd heard one of the old guys who frequented the cafe use. I nodded and tried to return the smile. Probably looked more like a snarl.

"It's OK," Alik said.

"I'd feel better if we mixed it up afterward," I said.

"I agree. That's why we will get him to take us to a car rental place after."

"Why don't you do that while I'm inside?"

"Even better," Alik said. "That way we waste no more time."

I glanced down at my watch. "Speaking of time. The bank open yet?"

Alik looked at the dash clock and nodded. He reached out, tapped the driver on the shoulder. They had a short exchange. The cabbie twisted the key in the ignition and crossed the lot. He stopped and waited while a group of homogeneous men passed by. Then we were on the road again.

Turned out we were more than five minutes from the bank.

Maybe Alik felt better further away from downtown. Could he have the same concerns over the phone as me?

The driver pulled into the parking lot and stopped in front of the square concrete building. A line of four people waited at the front door. I could see a banker on the other side of the smoky glass. She was slim and dressed in a dark dress. She reached out and twisted the lock. The door opened. The woman was smiling as she stepped aside and greeted each person in line as they walked inside.

"Shouldn't take long," I said. "Go ahead and get the car. Meet me out back."

Alik nodded. I opened the door and stepped out. He called after me, holding the phone out the window.

"Better you keep it," he said.

I walked back, grabbed it, and powered it down while I headed toward the entrance. It was warm already. And humid. The clouds bunched up overhead. They looked black in some spots. I figured it'd be raining when I stepped back outside. Hopefully they had a waterproof bag for me to use.

Cold air wrapped around me as I opened the door and crossed the threshold. My footsteps echoed off the tile floor. The walls in the entryway looked the same as the material used outside. Past that, they smoothed out and were painted an industrial grey. Similar looking short-pile color carpet butted up to the tile.

On the other side of the room were four teller windows. Two had signs in the middle which I assumed said closed. The other two were occupied by young women who looked like they might've been sisters. I glanced around the room. There were several offices with windows for walls. The woman who'd opened up the bank met my gaze and smiled. She stood as I approached.

I stopped in her doorway and said, "Do you speak English?"

She smiled and nodded and gestured for me to have a seat.

I pulled the door shut behind me. It banged as it latched. She was younger than she looked from a distance. The tight spirals of her hair bounced as she moved. Her thin nose had a slight crook to it, but nothing that took away from her looks. I sat opposite her and folded my hands on her desk.

"How may I assist you this morning, sir?" Her words were practiced but her pronunciation sounded forced. Better than I could do in her native tongue, that's for sure.

"I need to wire in some money from a Swiss account."

Her eyebrows rose and she cast a quick glance over me. I didn't match the profile of a customer who'd walk in and make such a request.

"I'm more comfortable dressed like this," I said, sparing her the embarrassment of questioning me.

She smiled. "I apologize. We don't have many of these types of requests. I'm not sure I know where to start."

I leaned forward, grabbed a pen and her notepad and wrote down the phone number to the bank. Underneath that I wrote the access code.

"That's all you'll need," I said. "Tell them you are calling to initiate a wire transfer. They'll patch you through to the correct person. Once you give that person the access code, they'll want to speak with me, then they'll need a bit more information from you. The money will be available a few minutes after that."

"I see you've done this before," she said.

"A time or two."

"Don't I need your name?"

I shook my head. Kept eye contact with her.

"Even for my own personal reference," she said.

I shrugged and told her my name was Martin. After that she stopped asking questions and placed the call. She left the phone on speaker. The operator answered and quickly transferred the call to the next department.

A voice came on and spoke in a neutral accent. "Access code."

She seemed taken aback that they hadn't greeted her. "Uh, well, it's—"

"Access code, please."

She read off the string of numbers and then repeated it upon request.

A few seconds passed. The connection hissed like a leaking tire.

"Place the account holder on the line."

I grabbed the phone, whispered, "Take me off speaker."

She hesitated.

"They're going to ask me specific questions. I can't have you knowing the answers."

She nodded knowingly, then pressed the speaker button.

"I'm here," I said.

The person on the other end read off five of the twenty possible security questions. I provided the prearranged answers. If anyone had heard the exchange, they'd be mystified by what we said. It was like two kids reading the scripts from ten different movies. That's how it had to be. The account had over five million in it and not even the bank in Switzerland could put a face to it.

"How much would you like transferred today, sir?"

"One hundred thousand U.S. dollars."

"Place the banker on the line please."

I handed the phone back to her. She set the cradle on her shoulder and held it in place with her cheek. It had the effect of bunching the skin up and narrowing her eye. She listened while the Swiss banker asked her for information, then she spat out a string of numbers and codes like she'd done this a hundred times. She thanked the person on the other end and set the phone on the cradle.

She looked at me with a smile. "Should be ready to go in a few minutes."

I was too tired to keep her engaged in conversation. She stood and walked around me and opened her office door. The low hum of chatter from the main room filtered in. I looked out past the glass wall. Six people stood in line. They spoke to one another while sipping their coffee. It was the kind of town where everyone knew each other. We couldn't be more than fifty miles from Athens. Yet the people here were very much small town.

Every few seconds she tapped her keyboard. Refreshing her screen, I presumed.

"And it's delivered." She stood and extended her hand. "Come with me, Mr., uh, Martin."

We walked into the lobby, past the tellers and the people waiting and the other offices. More than a few male eyes watched her as we passed. She pulled a key from her pocket and inserted it into a thick steel door that hissed when she opened it. The air inside was a little cooler, and a lot more stale. Almost smelled like a hospital.

She grabbed a metal briefcase the size of a large luggage bag. It had wheels on one end and a handle on the other. She fingered the combination lock.

"Do you have a preference?" she asked.

"For?" I said.

"Denominations."

"Mix it up evenly." I paused a beat and heard tinny thumps against the roof. The rain had started. "Would you happen to have a waterproof bag big enough to fit the case?"

She nodded without looking back and continued filling the briefcase. After she was finished she rose and gestured me further into the room. There was another door, this one not as domineering as the first. She used another key. I followed her into a small square room with a stainless steel table in the middle.

"I'll count," she said. "Then you do the same."

Less than ten minutes later, the briefcase was stuffed inside a large duffel bag, and she was shaking my hand outside her office. I thanked her, then turned and headed for the exit.

"Goodbye, Mr. Martin. Enjoy the rest of your stay."

There would be nothing enjoyable about it.

## 31

I FELT LIKE I WORE A TARGET THAT WAS VISIBLE FROM OUTER space. Standing in an unknown city behind a bank while holding a hundred grand wasn't the smartest thing I'd ever done. And I'd done plenty of stupid things. Alik had left me the phone, but kept the pistol.

Thirty minutes had passed. Had to be enough time to get a car and get back.

Then the what-ifs kicked in.

The police had found Esau's body sooner than we anticipated. Someone had mentioned we lived upstairs. We weren't there. Esau's car was gone. Two plus two equals four. Someone manages to get our images up and the cops spot Alik.

Or maybe there'd been an accident. I had the phone. Alik had no ID on him. No one would know who to contact if he were seriously injured.

"Stop it, Jack," I muttered.

I was wasting energy. Energy I didn't have to spare. The day might last another eighteen hours. Or it could be over in two. Either way, I had to conserve.

The rain had fallen hard for a few minutes, but then settled to a drizzle. Steam rose off the asphalt. Max humidity. Sweat coated my forehead, mixing with raindrops. I felt beads dripping down my neck and back.

It was a bad idea to hang around the back of the bank for too long. Especially carrying a large duffel bag. But I couldn't leave. Not until I saw or heard from Alik. So I looked around and spotted a bench tucked between a couple trees. Looked like a good enough spot.

I sat there for five minutes before a set of headlights flashed at me. The horn barked a couple times. The vehicle cut across the lot toward me, then whipped to the side. The driver's door opened and Alik stepped out.

"The hell took you so long?" I said.

"Three people ahead of me," he said. "You believe that? In this little place?"

I shook my head and said nothing.

"You get it?"

I held up the bag. "Right here."

"All of it?"

"And then some."

"What's the extra for?"

I shrugged. "We'll see."

I hopped in the car and opened the bag. I pulled out the extra cash and tucked it in the glove box.

"You think that's the safest place for it?"

"Got anywhere better?"

"No." Alik reached down and pulled out a pistol. "But I got this off my pilot friend. Didn't want you to have it while you were inside the bank."

I took the weapon and inspected it. It was a Jericho 941. A 9mm pistol popular with Israeli Special Forces. "What exactly did your friend do before ferrying his friends over the sea in his little Cessna?"

"A little of this. Little of that. Know what I mean?"

"Yeah, I know exactly what you mean."

We stopped at a light on the edge of town. "Should we call now?"

"Not yet. Let's drive past the house. Want to make sure I know where it is. We'll call then and loop back so he has no choice but to meet us there."

"Do we really want to do that?"

"I don't know. Part of me says it's the dumbest idea I've ever had, and believe me, there've been plenty of them. At the same time, I know he can find us back in town. Hell, he's probably got people still close by the cafe. I think every minute we waste is an opportunity for them to discover Esau's dead. So going direct to Kostas makes most sense."

Alik thinned his lips and stared at me for a long moment. "If you say so."

We continued on with only the wind rushing in through the cracked windows breaking the silence.

I looked over the map Alik had picked up with the rental. It took a few minutes, but I located the correct road. Alik studied the map, traced his course with his finger. For more than thirty minutes, we traversed the hilly, winding roads until we reached the airstrip I'd departed from the night before. A short drive later, we passed the obscure house that had contained half- or fully-nude women the night before, and led to a walkway that wound through landscaping on the way to Kostas's office. Two women were smoking in front of the entrance door. They had on tight shorts and shirts that were torn just above the navel. They ignored us as we passed.

"Turn around and pull over here," I said.

Alik jammed on the brakes. The car fishtailed on the slick road. He maintained control, veered hard to the side then whipped the vehicle around and stopped on the opposite shoulder.

"Time to make a call."

The phone had one number in its contact list. I highlighted it, pressed send, waited for the tones.

"Was wondering when we'd hear from you." The neutral accent gave the man on the other end of the line away as Chris. "The old man come up with the rest?"

"Isadora still in good condition?" I said. "Last I saw her, you were holding your pistol to her head."

"All for effect, my friend. Didn't harm a hair on that gorgeous head of hers."

"Put Kostas on."

"You are not in a position to demand such things, Noble."

I hated that he knew my name. The guy came from somewhere else. A hired mercenary. He'd go back where he came from at some point. He'd mention my name. Someone would recognize it. God forbid if Frank hadn't released me to the world by then.

Chris said, "We'll meet you—"

"We'll be at the house in two minutes," I said. "Call off the guards up front. I know the way to Kostas's office."

He started to say something. An objection, I figured. I pulled the phone away and ended the call.

"Sounds like that went well," Alik said.

"As well as expected," I said.

"Time to go?"

"Yeah, time to go."

## 32

No one stood outside when we pulled into the driveway. Presumably, Chris had sounded the alarm and someone told the women to get inside. Alik braked hard on the driveway. The car swerved into the grass. He left the engine running as we stepped out. The ground was muddy. Felt like the humidity rose up from the earth. Smelled similar to a wet dog. The house shielded us from the wind. It shook branches and leaves overhead. Sounded a bit like the rolling waves outside our window at the cafe.

I didn't bother knocking on the front door. Reached out and turned the knob. It was unlocked.

The girls had retreated inside. There were a few others in there with them. No guards, though. And there were no smiles or gestures with various body parts or winks this time. They covered themselves up with pillows or their own hands. Smoke leaked from a clear glass bong set on the couch to the right of the back door. The pungent odor of marijuana filled the room.

Weed and sex. I hoped that's what Kostas's crew had on their mind that morning.

I barreled through the back door and scanned the walkway. No one waited. They'd all headed for the boss's office, I presumed. We took the winding walkway cautiously, but not slowly. There was no smell of lavender. The wind blew it past and replaced it with the scent of rain and earth.

"How many you think there will be?" Alik said.

"There were at least eight here last night," I said.

"They'll want our weapons."

"Probably."

"Fuck that. We don't give them up."

"Works for me."

We passed the final curve and the backdoor was in sight. It opened when we were ten feet from it. The bald guy with the fat head and mustache stood there. He held the door open with one hand. A pistol with the other. His round frame blocked the entrance.

"That the money?" he said.

"Yeah," I said.

"Let me see it," he said.

"Piss off," Alik said.

"Who the hell is he?" the bald guy said.

"He's with me." I had my hand wrapped around the pistol's grip. "Now it's best you step back."

"Give up your weapons first."

I shook my head. "Not gonna happen."

"I'll shoot you right here then." He swung the handgun side to side. I noticed the whites of his eyes were glossy and stained red.

"How much of that weed you smoke back there?" I said.

He looked over his shoulder. Back at us.

"Room was a haze," Alik said. "You must be flying right now."

The bald guy lifted his weapon, but aimed it somewhere in between us.

"You couldn't hit the broad side of a barn," I said. "Lower your weapon and step back. If Kostas wants us unarmed, he can tell us himself."

The bald guy looked scared and confused and like he wanted to get back to the room and the ladies and the pot. He hopped from foot to foot as though he had to take a piss. Then he retreated into the hallway, pulling the door wide open.

It took a few seconds for my eyes to adjust to the dim light as I crossed the threshold. Once they did, I saw that it was empty except for my bald friend. Alik stepped in. The bald guy let go of the door. I drew back and punched him in the gut, grabbed his arm, wrenched the pistol away. He fell to the floor, hands clawing at the thick carpet as though the oxygen he needed to refill his lungs was there.

"Let's go," I said, tucking the extra pistol around my back in my waistband.

At the other end of the hallway I didn't bother to knock. I turned the knob, felt the latch give, and kicked the door open.

Kostas sat behind his overbearing desk, smiling. He didn't flinch when the door crashed wide on its hinges.

I swept the room left to right and back again. Isadora sat at a small circular table, facing away from me. Chris was on the other side of the room, hands crossed by his waist. His pistol dangled from his right hand. He nodded at me, then studied Alik for a long time after we entered the room.

"What's he doing here?" Kostas said.

"He's here for just in case," I said.

"In case of what?" Kostas rose slowly. He winced the way old men do when they stand. Pains left behind from a lifetime of action. "Are you saying I'm not a man of my word?"

"I trust no one, Kostas."

"Smart man," he said. "Neither do I."

"Where's the rest of your thugs?"

He shrugged. "It's early. Anyway, judging by what you did to Mikhail out there, they are worthless in the morning. Not like we get a lot of visitors out here. My reputation scares people a lot more than these morons do."

I smiled at him, but internally I was cataloguing everything in the room and matching it against what had been there the night before. Fatigue had set in. Things didn't look right. I didn't know if I could trust my memory.

Kostas's gaze traveled to the bag. "That the money?"

I nodded.

"All of it?" he said.

I nodded again.

"May we count it?"

"I want to talk to Isadora first."

"You can turn around," he said to her.

Her eyes were red and puffy. Her nose red and raw. Her bottom lip swollen on the left. I wondered if they knew about Esau already. Something had to account for the light mood and lack of security.

"You OK?" I said to her.

She nodded. "You?"

"Hanging in there."

"I'm sorry, Jack."

"Don't be. It's all right. We're gonna get you out of here soon."

She looked away for a few moments. Glanced back at me. Turned back in her chair.

"Now may we count it?" Kostas said.

I motioned with my head for Alik to join Isadora. The floor reverberated slightly as he stepped behind me. I drew the bag back and let its weight carry it forward. It arced through the air and hit the ground with a thud about halfway between me and Kostas.

His face drew tight, but relaxed soon enough. Getting your hands on almost a hundred grand you figured was lost had a way of doing that to a man. He gestured toward Chris, who stepped forward and scooped up the bag. He brought it to the old guy's desk, unzipped it, looked inside, shrugged, then dumped the contents out.

For ten minutes they sorted and piled and counted and recounted the money. Isadora sat still, facing the corner. Alik stood next to her, staring at the two men. I figured the bald guy was outside the door. Probably called a few more of Kostas's men and told them to get back. Ten minutes in, they were probably halfway there.

"We good?" I said.

Kostas looked up at me, over at Isadora, up at Chris.

"It's all here," he said.

"So we're done then," I said.

"We're done."

Alik grabbed Isadora's arm and pulled. She was dead weight. He leaned over and wrapped her arm around the back of his neck while threading his arm around her back. I stood by the door, waiting. He walked. Her feet dragged. What had they done to her? I thought I might have to return later to discuss it with Chris and Kostas.

I pulled the door open. The bald guy stood at the other end of the hall, looking at the ground. Alik pulled Isadora close and led her through the opening. I stepped out after them.

And then Kostas said, "One more thing."

## 33

It felt as though my internal temperature dropped fifteen degrees. My arms and legs went numb. My breath caught in my chest. The hallway tilted and spun. He wanted more. They always want more. I heard Chris rack his pistol's slide. Didn't have to look back to know he'd aimed it at my back.

"I have one more thing to ask you," Kostas said.

"Wait here," I said to Alik. "Anything happens, open fire and run."

"We're all real curious which one of you did it?"

I turned and stepped back into the room. Chris matched my pace, retreating backward. He did have his pistol out, but it wasn't aimed in my direction. It pointed perilously at the floor.

"Did what?" I said.

"Who took out Esau?"

Isadora choked back a sob. Alik said something to try to comfort her. Used a tone I'd never heard from him.

"Don't know what you're talking about," I said.

"Lies, lies," he said. "They only make me angry."

"You think I care if you're angry?"

"I think you should."

I said nothing.

A smile played on his face. Curled up on one end and slid to the other like a wave. Then it crashed. His mouth parted. Exposed his yellow teeth.

"I had a guy posted outside the cafe. He went in after you two left this morning. Found old Esau dead on his desk. A bloody note trapped under his head. Only my guy figures someone else fired the fatal shot."

"Why's that?"

"That is just what he told me."

"Your guy's an idiot."

"I could have told you that."

"If we had done it, the blood splatter would have been all over the desk, chair, lower wall, and floor. Wasn't like that. Bullet went in from down low, out the back of his head. Tore through the high back of his seat, and hit the wall four feet above his head. Blood hit mid-wall and traveled upward. Parts of his skull and brains were on the ceiling."

"He killed himself."

"Yeah, unless you had something to do with it."

"I wished my old friend no ill will."

I laughed. "You're kidding, right?"

"Well, so long as he delivered in time." He picked up a couple stacks of money and balanced them one in each hand. "And it turns out he did. Which makes his suicide all that more intriguing. Wouldn't you say?"

"I wouldn't presume to know what's going on in the mind of a depressed man. He lost his wife. Now he was going to lose his house, the cafe, possibly his niece. Too much to take, I guess."

The old guy stared at the money in his hands. Nodded.

"We done now?" I said.

"One more piece of business."

"Jesus Christ, what?"

"I ran your name."

"So?"

"Some interesting hits came back."

"And?"

"I think there might be some people interested in knowing your whereabouts."

I took a step to his desk. Kostas looked up. Chris stepped back. His pistol rose.

"Lots of Jack Nobles in the world, old man."

"True, but not many who match the description of the Jack Noble who died in prison in Russia last month. And at the same time, a Russian prison guard disappeared. Only it turns out they think the guard might have been an intelligence agent. A spy. And a double one, at that."

"What're you getting at?"

"I have friends around the globe, including some in Russia. People in the government who may or may not be on the right side of things. I think they might find it quite intriguing that a man sharing that same name and traveling with a Russian, who both show no fear in my presence, are here in Greece, hiding out in Crete."

"So pick up the phone then."

"Excuse me?"

"Quit fucking around with me. If you're gonna turn me over, then pick up the damn phone and make that call."

Laughing, Kostas stood, held out his arms. "Let's not get too far ahead of ourselves. I'm not going to make a call. I just wanted you to know, in case I come calling or something, that you should think twice about rebuffing me. And also to let you know that if something were to happen to me, procedures have been put in place to make sure that those friends of mine receive this information."

His face was like a stone wall with two dark eyes peering through. I held it for a few, and then looked down at the ground. Lifted my hands, clasped them around the back of my head.

"Be ready, Jack Noble," he said.

I let my arms drop, swooping to the side, then grabbed my wrist behind my back.

"Because I see myself needing your services very soon," he said.

The back of my hand rested against something cool and hard.

"And you better pick up and be ready to go when I ca—"

He didn't finish the sentence. I'd pulled the backup piece I took off of the bald guy with the fat head and mustache and opened fire on Kostas. Three red blossoms formed on his chest, tightly grouped at dead center. He fell backward into the bookcase. Several volumes rocked on the shelf and spilled over, landing on top of him. His wide-eyed stare lost focus and dimmed.

Behind me there was shouting. A shot was fired. The bald guy grunted and moaned. Alik fired a second shot and the other man went silent.

Chris stood less than eight feet from me. His arm dangled at his side. The gun pointed at the ground. He stared at Kostas, shaking his head.

I drew the other pistol, aimed both at him. He looked over at me.

"Dammit, Noble." The neutral accent was gone. I worked to place his voice. He threw his free hand in the air and held his thumb and index finger a fraction of an inch apart. "I was this fucking close. We almost had his entire support network, and you come along and fuck it up."

"The hell you talking about?" I kept both pistols aimed at him, but my mind was already racing through our exit. What if the bald guy had called in others? Every second we wasted meant more chance of a shootout.

Perhaps thinking the same thing, Alik said, "Jack, we need to go."

Chris holstered his pistol and walked over to Kostas. He leaned over. Grabbed a fistful of his own hair with each hand. He turned to me.

"Who are you?" I said.

"My name is Christopher Stoss and I'm a Mossad operative. I've been undercover here for three years, during which time I worked my way into Kostas's organization, and practically became his right hand man. All for the sole purpose of taking down his network because, among other things, they fund terrorists who wish to bring harm to my country."

I took a step back.

"Jack," Alik said. "Let's go."

"I can still salvage this." Chris stepped toward me. "Shoot me."

"What?"

"You can hit me without doing damage, right? If you are who I think you are, then I know you can." He turned his head away from his right shoulder. "Come on, Noble. You owe me this. If I'm not injured, they'll wonder why you left me. I'll have to abandon the op. Coming off under cover, you know what that means, don't you?"

"You'll be stuck in an office," I said.

"I'm not ready for that," he said.

"Jack!" Alik said. "We need to get out of here."

I lifted the pistol Alik had secured from his pilot friend. Aimed it at Chris.

He held up a finger. "Just so you know, I ever run into you again, I'm going to kill you."

I pulled the trigger. The bullet seared through the flesh of his shoulder. Through and through.

"Now get the hell out of here," he shouted.

# 34

We hurried down the walkway. Isadora had come to and needed little assistance. I led the way, both guns drawn, ready to fire. The back door of the front house opened. I waited until I had a clear view. Didn't want to shoot one of the women.

Michael stepped out, holding a bottle in one hand and a sandwich in the other. He stopped. Looked confused. Dropped his food and reached to his side.

I fired twice. Hit him in the gut. He fell over and rolled on his back. I rushed forward. Shot him again, this time in the chest.

There were screams from inside the house. A woman poked her head out. She stared at the dying man on the ground. She tried to slam the door shut, but it bounced back open, hitting her in the face. Her feet tangled as she tried to turn and run.

"Don't shoot me," she said, one arm outstretched toward me.

I stepped past her, into the room, and cleared it. A few women remained, that was it. They pulled their knees to their breasts and covered their faces with their hands, leaving gaps between fingers to watch me. I crossed the room and stopped at the front door, waited for Alik.

"Wait back there, Isadora," I said. "We both need to be ready, Alik."

Isadora remained at the back of the room as Alik joined me. He pulled the door open. I checked outside first. It was clear from there to the driveway. He pulled it wider. The rental car still idled on the grass.

"Let's go."

I stepped out front, aware of the heavy gusts that whipped over the top of the house. The trees shook. Leaves blew up and down and to each side. My feet sunk an inch in the muddy ground.

"We good out there?" Alik said.

"Yeah, come on."

We reached the rental and helped Isadora into the back seat. She folded her legs underneath her and crumbled to the side, resting her head on the sidewall. Alik and I got in. He backed into the driveway, the road, then shifted into first and peeled away. We didn't pass another car for at least three miles.

A few miles after that he pulled over and made a call.

"He'll be at the same air strip in two hours," Alik said.

I looked up at the streaming grey clouds. Rain had started falling again. "Any other options?"

"Ferry will be rough. And it takes a long time. And we still might have to wait two hours."

"All right, let's get close and find someplace quiet to pull over and wait."

Thirty minutes later we parked in a small clearing, shielded from the wind gusts. Raindrops hammered the roof.

"Your money," Alik said.

"What about it?" I said.

"You left it behind."

"Figured that might keep them out of our hair. Plus, the whole thing with Chris threw me off. The whole time, I thought there was something different about him. Figured him for a merc, you know. Guy like us. Goes into business doing security work."

Alik nodded and said nothing.

"Turns out he was more. I mean, I see why he never let on. But, damn, what are the odds?"

Alik shrugged. "I guess we need to call Frank now."

"Why?"

"Because of what Kostas said about notifying people if something happened to him. I still can't believe you pulled the trigger after that."

"As opposed to what? Being his bitch?"

"But now they might come after us."

"No one's coming after us."

"How can you be certain?"

"Because Kostas was bluffing me."

"You know this how? The way he smiled or blinked or held his hands?"

"Nothing that scientific," I said. "Just a guess."

"I'm calling Frank."

"You can't call him."

"Yes, I can."

"What are you gonna tell him? About all this?"

Shaking his head, Alik slammed his fist into the steering wheel. "Shit, I can't tell him."

"If they come, they come, Alik. We'll deal with it then."

A while later we received the call from Alik's friend. We ditched the car at the gate and were airborne ten minutes later. The flight wasn't smooth, but we made it back.

Isadora spoke for the first time when we were back in her uncle's car. All she said was she wanted to go home. Esau's house wasn't safe, but she wouldn't hear our argument. I offered her a pistol, but she refused. Feared that in her current mental state, she might do something stupid. I told her I'd come by in the morning to check on her.

The cafe was wrapped in police tape. They spotted us when we arrived, pulled us inside, asked us a bunch of questions. We stuck to a story of heading out for a fishing trip that was canceled due to the weather. Took some time to get back home. The local cops seemed to accept our story and let us go up to the apartment.

I staggered into my room and collapsed on the bed. Slept straight through to the next morning. After waking, I fixed a pot of coffee, drained a mug, then set off to see Isadora, like I promised. Found the front door unlocked and the house empty. She left a note saying she couldn't stay around any longer and had gone home, wherever that was.

For three days, Alik and I were prisoners in the apartment. The police were in and out. Repairmen came along and replaced the front window. We grew so bored that we went down and cleaned the cafe up after Esau's death was ruled a suicide and the cops were done with the place.

Almost a week later, we'd reopened the cafe and let the old guys in to hang out and play their game. I was sitting by the front door, drinking coffee and eating eggs and lamb when a familiar face showed up. Almost too familiar. Thought I was looking at Esau's ghost.

The guy pulled the door open, stopped and looked at me. "You the guy that got the cafe up and running again?"

I nodded.

"Jack?"

I nodded again.

"Heard about you from Esau's niece."

"That's great," I said. "Who are you?"

"Nic," he said. "Esau's brother."

"Twins?"

"Nah. Couple years apart. At this age, doesn't matter much."

"Thought his brother was dead."

"That's our older brother. He was a couple years older than me."

"You here to collect his things?"

Nic shook his head. His gaze danced around the place. "Esau left this to me."

"What's there to leave? The bank'll probably take it soon."

"Why? Did he have debt I don't know about? Wouldn't the lawyer have known?"

"Debt? This was his debt. This and the house. He had nothing."

Nic laughed. "Son, he owned this place and the house free and clear."

"Son of a bitch," I muttered.

"What?"

"Nothing." I stood. "Let me show you to the office."

Later that day, after the old men had gone home, and Nic had a handle on things, I retreated to the terrace and caught the final rays of the sun before it dipped behind the buildings. I stared out at the water, watching the colors shift and soften to black.

The door opened behind me. Soft footsteps crossed the tiles toward me. They echoed off the walls. A hand touched my shoulder. Squeezed gently. I looked down at the long, slender fingers. Lavender enveloped me.

"I had to come say goodbye," Isadora said, stepping around my side, dragging her nails across the back of my neck. She sat in the chair opposite me.

"I'm glad you did." I held her gaze for a second. "Where're you going?"

"Away, for a while. Then hopefully back to school."

"I have something for you. Wait here." I headed inside, up the stairs, into the apartment, then back again. She was sitting in the same spot and smiled when I stepped outside.

"What is it?" She pointed at the bag I held.

"Something for you. It's what was left over from the money…" I didn't finish the sentence.

Isadora did. "You got for Kostas."

I nodded. "How are you doing with that?"

"It's not easy. Bad dreams every night. But, it is what it is. Right?"

"Suppose so." I handed her the bag.

"How much is it?"

"Enough to get you started at school."

She set it on the table and stood and fell into me. Her arms wrapped around my neck. Her fingers ran through my hair. Her lips met mine. I held her there for a long minute. Neither of us wanted to let go. I wasn't sure what we represented to one another, but it felt good. She released me. I collapsed in my chair. She backed away, smiling.

"Now your turn to wait," she said.

I nodded as she hurried across the tiles, her steps echoing into a jumbled mess. The door opened, then whooshed shut.

And I waited.

A minute. Five. Ten. Half an hour. Two hours later, she still hadn't returned. She'd left everything perfect.

In a way.

## 35

THE ESTATE LAWYER RECOGNIZED THE SIGNIFICANCE OF HIS DEAD client and all that he possessed, so he contacted his most trusted broker, who then sent out the twenty-eight year old man with explicit instructions to sort everything, but get rid of nothing.

So the man left early on a Wednesday morning, making the trek from Athens to the house in the hills. He pulled out the keys that had been delivered to him the night prior and opened the front door. *The hell*, he thought, looking around the trashed room with the tacky couches and empty booze bottles and marijuana pipes and ladies undergarments strewn about.

He went right through that room, out the back door, finding peace along the walkway.

"What is that?" he muttered to himself, closing his eyes, inhaling deeply. "Jasmine? No, lavender."

His mother's favorite. Perhaps he'd pick some on the way out.

He reached the building in back and made his way in and down the hall and into a splendid office. The furniture was exquisite. The book collection was huge and looked older than the obvious antique desk.

What other treasures did the office hold?

He started with the desk, went through it drawer by drawer. He reached the last one, which contained only one item. A large tan envelope, made out to an address written in Cyrillic font. A piece of paper was taped to the envelope and it said that should something have happened to the owner of the house that reeked of foul play, the letter was to be mailed.

The guy held the envelope for a long time. He didn't want to sort it because sorting it meant that he'd have to put it in a pile and the pile it belonged in meant it would go in the trash.

Now, the guy ignored the last part, the part about foul play, even though he knew the owner of the estate had met a gruesome death. Instead his romantic mind raced to other possibilities. That the guy who'd died had harbored a secret love and had never told the woman.

He couldn't let that letter go to waste. No way.

So he crossed the room with the envelope in hand. He picked up his bag. Unzipped it. Stuffed the letter inside. And later that day, as he headed home after a long day of sorting and piling and deciding which stuff might get tossed and which should be sold, he stopped by a Hellenic Post office and slipped the envelope in the mail.

"Good luck," he said, looking up. *A stupid thing to say*, he thought. And then he had reservations. Maybe some things were better left unsaid. Maybe that letter would destroy the bond of a happy family. There might be unintended consequences, no matter how noble his intentions had been.

***THE END***

Jack Noble's story continues in *Noble Retribution (Jack Noble #6)* - Link and excerpt below!

Want to be among the first to download the next Jack Noble book? Sign up for L.T. Ryan's newsletter, and you'll be notified the minute new releases are available - and often at a discount for the first 48 hours! As a thank you for signing up, you'll receive a complimentary copy of *The Recruit: A Jack Noble Short Story*.

Join here: http://ltryan.com/newsletter/

I enjoy hearing from readers. Feel free to drop me a line at ltryan70@gmail.com. I read and respond to every message.

If you enjoyed reading *When Dead in Greece*, I would appreciate it if you would help others enjoy these books, too. How?

**Lend it.** This e-book is lending-enabled, so please, feel free to share it with a friend. All they need is an amazon account and a Kindle, or Kindle reading app on their smart phone or computer.

**Recommend it.** Please help other readers find this book by recommending it to friends, readers' groups and discussion boards.

**Review it.** Please tell other readers why you liked this book by reviewing it at your favorite bookseller, or Goodreads. Your opinion goes a long way in helping others decide if a book is for them. Also, a review doesn't have to be a big old book report. A few words is sufficient. If you do write a review, please send me an email at ltryan70@gmail.com so I can thank you with a personal email.

**Like Jack.** Visit the Jack Noble Facebook page and give it a like: https://www.facebook.com/JackNobleBooks.

<<<<>>>>

# ALSO BY L.T. RYAN

## The Jack Noble Series

The Recruit (free)

The First Deception (Prequel 1)

Noble Beginnings

A Deadly Distance

Ripple Effect (Bear Logan)

Thin Line

Noble Intentions

When Dead in Greece

Noble Retribution

Noble Betrayal

Never Go Home

Beyond Betrayal (Clarissa Abbot)

Noble Judgment

Never Cry Mercy

Deadline

End Game

## Mitch Tanner Series

The Depth of Darkness

Into The Darkness

Deliver Us From Darkness - coming soon

## **Affliction Z Series**

Affliction Z: Patient Zero

Affliction Z: Abandoned Hope

Affliction Z: Descended in Blood

Affliction Z Book 4 - Spring 2018

# NOBLE RETRIBUTION: CHAPTER 1

Jack Noble reached out and grabbed the thin handle of the white mug on the edge of the table. He brought it to his lips and blew into the cup, sending a cloud of steam into his eyes and nose. The smell of strong coffee invaded his senses and alerted his body to the rush of caffeine that would soon come. He placed his lips to the cup and pulled a half mouthful of the hot liquid in, letting it cool under his tongue before swallowing. He watched the morning sun crest over the Libyan Sea in the Mediterranean. Orange, red, pink and purple colored the sky and sea, making it impossible to tell where one ended and the other began.

He knew that the cropping of white buildings behind him changed colors with every passing minute as if they were part of a laser light show. Some mornings he walked on the beach and watched the town during sunrise. Other mornings he sat on the small cafe's patio and woke up with the sea.

The small town of Palaiochora on the Greek island of Crete

had turned out to be the perfect hiding spot for a man who was now a ghost. Small. Quiet. Quaint. Tourists came through daily. Some stayed overnight. Most didn't. Only a few of them ever came into the cafe. The cafe with the apartment above it. The apartment that Jack lived in with Alik, the Russian.

"Good morning, Jack."

Jack nodded, keeping his eyes fixed on the sea and his coffee mug in front of his mouth.

"Beautiful morning." Alik's Russian accent had started to take on a Greek quality over the past few weeks.

"Just like every morning the last six months," Jack said.

Six months. The most peaceful six months of Jack's adult life. After sixteen years of non-stop action, Jack's now thirty-six year old body welcomed the respite. But the itch had returned. The calm and quiet of Palaiochora had started to wear on him. He missed the city. He missed the action and the thrill of his job. In addition to that, there was too much unfinished business. Professionally and personally.

Jack held the mug to his face with both hands. He took a sip. When he exhaled, his breath turned to steam as it met the cool morning air. A breeze blew in from across the sea. The air bit at his face with the promise of a mild spring day. He set his mug down on the table. Pushed the sleeves of his blue sweater past his forearms. Grabbed a napkin and wiped droplets of coffee away from the hair on his upper lip. He rubbed his face, feeling the coarse hair that covered his cheeks and chin. His hair, uncut for six months, hung over his forehead, past his eyebrows. He used both hands to part it in the middle and brushed it back.

"Have you heard from Frank?" asked Jack.

Alik shook his head. "I'll try him today." He cut a piece of danish with a butter knife and stabbed it with a fork. "You are a ghost, Jack. They want to keep it that way. If it takes a year to get you off this island, then it takes a year."

Jack sighed. He arched his back and stretched his arms high in the air. A ghost, he thought. Frank did Jack a favor when he had Alik temporarily kill him while he was imprisoned in the Russian hell hole nicknamed *Black Dolphin*. Jack still had no idea how they pulled it off. Alik wouldn't tell him and Jack hadn't talked to Frank yet. Not one to dwell on such things, Jack had almost forgotten all about it.

Jack pushed back in his chair, stood and walked to the green painted metal railing at the far end of the patio. The railing could use a fresh coat of paint. He leaned over and looked down into the blue sea. Then he turned around and leaned back against the long cold strip of metal. He reached into his pocket for a cigarette. There weren't any there. Hadn't been for three months. Old habits die hard, he figured.

"I'm sure it will be soon," Alik said.

"You said that three months ago."

Alik shrugged. "What do you want me to say? Quit asking."

Jack waved him off and leaned his head back. Over the top of the cafe he could see a few of the houses built into the hillside. The sunrise color show was ending and the buildings were fading from orange to white.

"What about me? He tell you what is going to happen to me yet?"

"Jack," Alik paused a second. "There isn't anything that I can—"

"Anything that you can divulge to me at this time. Yeah, I know." Jack crossed the patio and leaned against the cool exterior wall of the building. His eyes shifted from Alik to the vast openness of the empty sea. "I wish you would quit this act and tell me. You said yourself, I'm a ghost. They wouldn't care about that if they didn't have plans for me. Well, let me tell you something, Alik. I have plans for me. I have some unfinished business that I need to attend to."

Jack stood there shaking his head for a minute before sitting down at the table, across from Alik.

The Russian placed both hands on the table and leaned forward. "Jack, yes, you are correct. They have a plan for you. I'm not privy to all the information, though. I promise you that."

An hour passed and they sat in silence. Jack drank two more cups of coffee and had a breakfast of eggs and fried kalitsounia, a sweet cheese pastry. The locals filed in and out of the cafe, grabbing the coffee and pastries they required to start their morning. A few of the old timers took regular seats on the patio, nodding at Jack as they passed. He thought he could get used to the life here. Not now. But someday. Someday when he had someone to share it with.

"What was that?" Alik asked.

Jack shrugged.

"Listen."

Jack leaned forward. Closed his eyes. He blocked out the chatter of the locals and honed in on a single voice. A voice that stood out from the rest. Similar to Alik's, but with a harsher tone. The voice rose and fell as it interrogated outside the cafe. And then inside.

"Russians."

Alik's eyes widened and he nodded in agreement.

From inside the cafe a voice called out in English, "Jack Noble. Present yourself now."

# NOBLE RETRIBUTION: CHAPTER 2

"Tell them to leave." Jack pointed at the locals seated at tables on the patio.

Alik spoke in Greek and then repeated in English, "Get off the patio. Through the cafe. Leave now, your lives are in danger."

Six older men looked around in confusion.

"Now," Alik shouted.

The men stood and staggered back through the door into the cafe. Coffee and coats and smokes in hand.

The patio offered Jack and Alik little in the way of cover or protection. Walled on three sides and open to the sea on the fourth with only the green metal railing separating the men from the water below. And with the air temperature at fifty degrees, the water would be too cold to offer a suitable means of escape. Besides, it was too shallow.

Jack scanned the tables. He grabbed two serrated edged knives and flipped them in his hands so that the blades pressed against his forearms. He nodded to Alik and flattened himself against the wall, a few feet from the door. Alik moved to the far end of the patio so that he would be the first man the Russian would see. Only just then Jack heard a second Russian voice. Possibly even a third. His eyes widened and he tried to get Alik's attention, but the man appeared to have already seen what Jack had heard.

Alik reached behind his back. Was he armed today? Both of the men had reached a point where they felt there weren't any real threats in the small town. Hell, on the entire island, for that matter. The chance of something happening seemed *less than* slim-to-none. Who would look for Jack, a man believed to be dead, at the southernmost point of Crete?

A voice called through the door. His voice sounded close, perhaps just past the threshold. Jack held the knives tight. One back against his left forearm ready to defend. The other pointing out ready to strike and attack. He thought about swinging his body around and launching himself through the door, attacking the first person he saw. He quickly shook the thought from his head. He felt rusty. No action for six months had dulled his responses and reflexes, and his senses were now overwhelmed. He closed his eyes and let the cool air rush in through his mouth. Lungs expanded and oxygen flooded his bloodstream. His mind calmed as he tensed and relaxed his muscles.

The first man stepped through the doorway. He focused on Alik and started toward him with his arms slightly extended.

Alik spoke in Russian. Jack didn't know what he said, but it obviously caught the other man's attention because he didn't even seem to notice Jack.

The second man stepped through. Jack wasted no time. He

turned and brought his right arm across his body with the blade of the knife extended. The man reacted and took a defensive position. He must have seen Jack in his peripheral vision. Unfortunately for the man, his reaction left the soft spot of his neck exposed. Jack adjusted his aim in a fraction of a second and plunged the knife deep into the man's neck. The sharp point combined with the force of Jack's blow allowed the knife to penetrate through the tangle of skin and muscle and blood vessels and finally into his spinal column. The blade severed the thread that linked the man's brain to his body. He dropped to the ground in a lifeless heap.

The first man through the door spun on his heels and reached inside his coat. The jacket fell open, revealing a pistol, most likely the Russian Army issued Makarov PMM. Jack couldn't be sure as he only saw the weapon for a split second. The moment the man's hand hit the handle of the gun, Jack leapt into the air. He swung his left arm in an arc. The dull side of the blade of the knife pressed against the side of his forearm. The serrated edge faced out. Jack timed the swing of his arm so that the knife sliced across the man's throat. The cut wasn't clean, but it did the job.

The Russian dropped his gun and brought both hands to his neck. It muffled, but didn't stop, the arterial spray. He backed into the center wall and slowly slid down it and into a seated position. Two thin lines of blood left an extended outline of his neck on the wall.

Jack allowed his momentum to carry him through his jump. He hit the ground and rolled on his back and then over onto his hands and knees. He got to his feet and rose to a standing position. He faced the open doorway between the cafe and the patio.

A third man yelled from inside the cafe. Jack scanned the room and saw the man aiming a gun in his direction. Jack quickly moved out of the man's sights. An explosion ripped through the air. A flash of light that lasted barely a second brightened the opening between the cafe and the patio. The bullet hit with a thud.

Alik groaned loudly and fell back into the wall. He shuffled his feet and fell to his left, trying to stay low and out of range of another shot.

Jack rushed toward the door. He was greeted by the sight of pandemonium inside the cafe. That told him that the third Russian would not be able to get a clean shot at him or Alik. But it also meant that he could possibly kill an innocent bystander with another shot. Jack blew through the open doorway.

Two older men had the Russian by his arms. A third older man had his thick arms wrapped around the Russian's neck. The Russian pushed back and tried to crush the older man on his back against the glass display case. They had not managed to get his gun from him, though, and he struggled to aim it in Jack's direction.

Jack continued toward the group of men and slammed his right fist in the Russian's jaw. The man went slack in the arms of the Greek men and his gun fell to the floor. Jack scooped the gun off the ground. Tucked it in his waistband. He grabbed a fistful of the man's hair and started pulling him toward the patio.

"That'll be enough," he said. "Thank you, gents."

Jack dragged the Russian onto the patio. He dropped him on the ground and then turned and slammed the door shut.

Alik had propped himself up against the wall. Blood poured from a bullet hole in his chest.

"Christ," Jack said. "Alik, you with me?"

Alik nodded slowly. He tried to speak.

"Save your strength."

Jack turned to the Russian. Kicked him in the stomach. The man rolled over and opened his eyes.

"Who sent you?" Jack said.

"Screw you," the Russian said in English.

Jack kicked him again.

"Who? Tell me or so help me I'll put a bullet in your head."

The man spit.

Jack knew this was a wasted effort. He needed to attend to Alik before he bled out. He knelt down and placed the barrel of the gun to the man's forehead.

"Last chance."

The man said nothing.

Jack cursed at the man. Pulled the trigger twice. The bullets ripped through the Russian's skull, tearing his brain apart.

Jack got up and went to the door. He opened it and yelled into the cafe.

"I need help out here."

The three older Greek men responded and came out to the patio. Two went to work on Alik. The third turned to Jack.

"We are all experienced medics," he said in English. "From the war."

Jack didn't ask which war. "Is he going to be OK?"

"We need to take him somewhere."

"Hospital won't be safe. There could be more of them." Jack gestured toward the three slain men on the patio.

"I know a place." The older man turned to his two friends and waved at Jack. "Come. Help. Get him to the truck."

∾

They drove through town and into the country. Fast and steady. Paved roads gave way to packed dirt. The truck slowed down. They turned onto a gravel driveway that jutted out between two lines of trees. A small stone house sat at the end of the driveway.

Jack turned to the man in the back of the truck sitting opposite him. Alik lay between them.

"Where are we?"

"My mother's house."

"She a doctor?"

"No." He paused a moment and looked toward the house. "I am, though."

The truck stopped near the house. The two Greek men in the cab got out and rushed to the rear of the vehicle. The four of them lifted Alik from the bed of the truck and carried him to the house. An old white haired lady with a slightly hunched back stood by the door, holding it open. They brought Alik inside and into the kitchen. Placed him on a long wooden table that looked to be over a hundred years old. The table was covered in white sheets. Several stainless steel medical tools were laid out neatly at one end.

The man who had declared himself a doctor grabbed a pair of scissors and cut Alik's shirt down the middle. He pried the blood-soaked garment from Alik's chest. The doctor wiped away blood from the site of the wound and inspected the damage.

"I think he's going to be OK. He's severely injured, but will heal."

Jack nodded and took a few steps back. He wanted to get

out of the way. The doctor knew what he was doing and the men appeared to have worked with him before. Jack, on the other hand, was useless in this situation.

Jack said, "His pocket. The phone."

The doctor nodded to one of the other men who reached into Alik's pocket and pulled out a cell phone. The man tossed it to Jack.

Jack snatched the phone mid-air and turned to the front door. He passed the white haired lady and stepped through the open doorway. He worked the phone. Pressed a button and scanned through a list until he found Frank's number. He highlighted the number and pressed send.

Frank answered midway through the third ring. "Hello?" His voice was soft and deep. He had been sleeping. Jack looked at his watch and calculated it was two in the morning on the east coast of the U.S.

"What did you do?"

"Huh? Who is this?" Frank's voice trailed off. Jack figured he was looking at his caller ID.

"Alik, huh? Jack, is that you?"

"What did you do, Frank?"

"Jack, what are you talking about?"

"God dammit, don't screw with me. I'll end you if you don't tell me the truth."

"I've been working to get you moved. I have it all set up for—"

"How did they know?"

"—two weeks from now. There's gonna be a guy…wait. How did who know what?"

Jack said nothing. He held the phone to his ear. He exhaled fast and heavy.

"Jack, what happened?"

"We were ambushed. This morning. At the cafe where we've been staying."

"Who?"

"Russians."

The line went silent and for a moment Jack thought Frank had hung up.

"This is bad, Jack. Very bad."

"No kidding, Frank. Alik's been injured. What are you going—"

"Hold on. I'm thinking."

Jack turned around and looked past the old woman in the doorway. Two men held Alik down while the doctor worked on his chest. It looked like he had forceps inserted into the wound in an effort to retrieve the bullet. Jack lowered his eyes toward the white haired woman. She held up a cigarette. He shook his head, shrugged and then held out his hand. The old woman lit the cigarette and handed it to him. The first drag tasted like the street after Mardi Gras and the smoke burned his lungs. He nearly coughed. But he took a second drag, and then a third. The rush of nicotine excited and then calmed him all within a period of twenty seconds.

"Christ," Jack muttered under his breath, disappointed in himself for accepting the cigarette.

"What?" Frank asked.

"Nothing," Jack said.

"Jack, call me back in five minutes. I need to wake someone up."

Jack looked around, through the trees, toward the dirt road leading in. Five minutes wouldn't be long enough to get someone else here to finish the job the three Russians failed to complete.

"OK. I'll call back in five."

He hung up the phone, took a final drag off the cigarette and dropped it to the ground where he crushed it with his heel. He walked past the woman in the doorway, nodding with a smile as he did so.

"How is he?"

The doctor looked over his shoulder. His hands continued to work, sewing shut the hole in Alik's chest.

"He'll live. The bullet lodged in his rib. The rib is broken. Shattered. But had it not stopped the bullet, your friend would be dead."

Jack stood next to the table. Looked down at Alik. The man's eyes fluttered as he passed between states of consciousness and unconsciousness. The doctor had given him some type of anesthetic, but Jack questioned its effectiveness.

"He'll be OK," the doctor said. "He should be in the hospital, though."

"Can't. You saw what happened at the cafe. He checks into a hospital, he won't check out."

"Then he can stay here," the old woman said.

The doctor nodded. "I'll keep an eye on him over the next few days. Administer pain meds so he isn't suffering. In a few days he should be in much better shape."

Jack looked at his watch and pulled the phone back out. He dialed the number as he walked toward the front door.

Frank answered after the first ring.

"Jack, OK. We're getting you out. I'm sending one of my guys."

"Just me," Jack said.

"What do you mean? Is Alik dead?"

"No, but he's in no condition to travel."

"Dammit. OK, I'm sending an extra man to stay with him then."

Jack looked back at the three Greek men and the old woman. "Probably a good idea."

"Where are you?"

"About ten miles outside of town. Get your men here and call me. I'll send a car."

"They'll be there by nightfall."

Click Here to Purchase Noble Retribution!

# ABOUT THE AUTHOR

L.T. Ryan is a *USA Today* and international bestselling author. The new age of publishing offered L.T. the opportunity to blend his passions for creating, marketing, and technology to reach audiences with his popular Jack Noble series.

Living in central Virginia with his wife, the youngest of his three daughters, and their three dogs, L.T. enjoys staring out his window at the trees and mountains while he should be writing, as well as reading, hiking, running, and playing with gadgets. See what he's up to at http://ltryan.com.

**Social Medial Links:**

- Facebook (L.T. Ryan): https://www.facebook.com/LTRyanAuthor

- Facebook (Jack Noble Page): https://www.facebook.com/JackNobleBooks/

- Twitter: https://twitter.com/LTRyanWrites

- Goodreads: http://www.goodreads.com/author/show/6151659.L_T_Ryan

CPSIA information can be obtained
at www.ICGtesting.com
Printed in the USA
BVHW031050280519
PP9964900001B/2/P